His name is

PATRICK DAWLISH

He is a very large man, with vast
shoulders that his well-cut suit cannot
conceal. But for the broken nose, a
legacy of an early battle in the boxing
ring, he would be as handsome as he
is massive . . .

He is always jumping in with both
feet where the police fear to tread.
And no thief, blackmailer or murderer
ever comes up against a tougher, more
resourceful, deadlier enemy than

PATRICK DAWLISH

Also by John Creasey

and published by Corgi Books

John Creasey
as
Gordon Ashe

Two Men Missing

CORGI BOOKS
TRANSWORLD PUBLISHERS LTD

A National General Company

TWO MEN MISSING

A CORGI BOOK 0 552 08825 0

Originally published in Great Britain
by John Long Ltd.

PRINTING HISTORY
John Long edition published 1943
Corgi revised edition published 1971

This book is set in Monotype Times

Corgi Books are published by Transworld Publishers Ltd.,
Cavendish House, 57–59 Uxbridge Road,
Ealing, London, W.5.
Made and printed in Great Britain by
Hunt Barnard Printing Ltd., Aylesbury, Bucks.

Two Men Missing

Chapter 1

Major Dawlish is Reluctant

'But why pick on me?' asked Patrick Dawlish.

'Well, you're so solid,' declared Amelia, smiling up at him warmly. 'You are, you know, and I don't mean that physically, although goodness knows – how much do you weigh?' She made the digression with another warm, encompassing smile.

'A little more than fourteen.'

'And I know you're six feet one inch and a bit,' declared Amelia, 'because you're exactly the same height as my father. It must be comforting to be a big man. You're very wide, too, aren't you?'

'Yes, I'm wide,' he assured her, 'although I've never been measured as far as I can remember. If it weren't for my nose, I would be quite good-looking. Such a pity –'

'Do you know, I think you're making fun of me,' said Amelia, her smile disappearing and her wide-set, lovely eyes, as blue as Dawlish's, regarding him with gentle, pained reproach. 'Pat, I thought I could rely on you to be serious.'

'The risk was yours,' Dawlish assured her, without smiling.

Amelia contemplated him for several seconds, and then her lips curved as she allowed her famous smile to dawn again. It was often said that neither man nor woman could resist Amelia Shortt when she turned her smile towards them and allied it to a request, no matter how outrageous the request might be. Amelia was twenty-two and beautiful, but her beauty was as naught compared to the charm of her smile.

She tried again, a note almost of wheedling in her voice.

'Pat, darling, please don't joke. I know you've only a short weekend, but it won't take you very long, and you're just the man to solve it.'

Had anyone but Amelia Shortt implored his aid Dawlish

would have declined; at the moment he was tired, and disinclined to mental effort; but there was the famous smile.

'You know very well that everyone regards you as an oracle,' Amelia went on. 'If you needed to earn money, or anything like that' – her hand flicked the air, at the impossibility that Dawlish would ever be in such a predicament – 'you would only have to open an office and put: "Patrick Dawlish, Private Detective" on the door, and you'd be crowded out with clients. I think you're wonderful.'

Dawlish narrowed his eyes and a deeper note entered his voice.

'Amy, no one else I know would dare to be as blatantly ingenuous as you, or so naive, or so innocent. But if I must stir myself for you, don't make it honey-sweet. I know perfectly well that the only person in this wide world whom you think is wonderful is Amelia Shortt. Shall we start from there?'

'You know, you're very nearly rude,' said Amelia, regarding him through long, dark lashes. 'If I didn't want your help so much I think I'd ignore you for the rest of the weekend. Do you ever talk to Felicity like that?'

'No,' said Dawlish lazily. 'Never.'

Amelia's smile of amusement was not quite up to her normal standard.

She shrugged.

'Let's be serious for a moment.' She leaned forward. 'Pat, my father is being blackmailed.'

Dawlish had been given to understand that she needed his assistance, but the calm assurance and matter-of-factness with which she delivered this statement startled him out of his habitual poise.

'Say that again,' he said.

'I knew it would interest you,' said Amelia with satisfaction. 'You see what a mistake you would have made if you'd refused to help?' She pouted a little, provocatively. 'You will do something, won't you?'

Dawlish's hand groped for his pipe.

'Tell me all,' he said.

'Bless you, Pat!'

Head thrown back, white, slender throat stretched so that her small, pointed chin was thrust forward, Amelia watched him from narrowed eyes and waited until his pipe was drawing smoothly.

8

The leaves of the beech tree rustled in a gentle wind. From the road the hum of traffic provided an unceasing background of noise, for Clay House, in spite of its beeches and chestnuts and fine lawns, was in fact in the middle of London.

'Father's been worried for some time,' continued Amelia at last, 'but I haven't known why. He just *won't* talk to anyone about his troubles, you know, he lives in a world of his own and I don't think he notices people. A week ago I discovered that he wasn't sleeping at night. His light is on until four or five in the morning, and I hear him walking about. Pat,' she went on dramatically, 'I don't think he's slept a wink for at least ten days!'

'Come, come,' said Dawlish lazily. 'That's hard to believe. I talked to him for half-an-hour this afternoon, and I would have noticed the signs of sleepless nights.'

'Do you mean you don't believe me?' ejaculated Amelia.

'Roughly, yes,' said Dawlish.

'But –' She looked amazed. 'I tell you that he hasn't even been to bed! Jameson, his man, told me that the bed hasn't been slept in for nearly a week. And if he hasn't been to bed he can't have been to sleep.'

Dawlish smiled amiably.

'There are such things as armchairs, you know.'

'Oh, nonsense!' exclaimed Amelia, heatedly. 'He may have managed to get forty winks now and again, but – he *is* being blackmailed. If you tell me that you don't believe me I shall –' She paused.

'Where's the evidence?' demanded Dawlish.

'It was last night,' said Amelia shortly. 'He was in the study late again, and I couldn't sleep. So I went down to remonstrate with him, and I heard voices. The door was ajar, and a man was speaking to Father, a man I've never seen before. He said –' Amelia half-closed her eyes, as one recalling a scene. "If you don't bring it, every penny of it, tomorrow night, I'll blow the gaff". It couldn't be more categorical than that, could it? I heard the man and saw him – he was a rather big fellow with dark, oily hair. Well, do you believe me now?' Her gaze became direct and challenging.

It was on the tip of Dawlish's tongue to tell her that he did not. He felt convinced that she had made up that quota-

9

tion. He allowed that there might have been a stranger in Shortt's room, and that some kind of threat might have been uttered, but he considered that as by no means established.

The one thing evolving from this unexpected conversation was that Amelia wanted his help; particularly for that night. Nothing was less pleasant a prospect, for of all things he felt that he needed sleep. Even then he had the utmost difficulty to keep his eyes open.

Whether Amelia was telling the truth or whether she had invented the story solely to arouse his interest, he did not know.

As she regarded him, her poise of youthful ingenuousness was forgotten. He had the impression that she was more than a little afraid lest he should refuse to believe her.

'And what happened when the man saw you?'

'Oh, but he didn't!' exclaimed Amelia. 'Our house is one of those unexpected ones, full of unnecessary alcoves and big pieces of furniture. I hid behind one of them until the man left. Then I started to follow him, but he went so quickly that he was out of the house before I was at the foot of the stairs. So' – Amelia paused again, then added with a flash of inspiration – 'It was so dark outside that I knew it was useless to try to find out where he'd gone. And when I went back, the study was locked.'

Dawlish said slowly: 'Is this gospel truth, or are you embellishing it?'

'It's gospel truth,' said Amelia very promptly, and without batting an eye.

'Then what do you want me to do?'

'Well, I thought perhaps you'd spend the night at our place, and then when Father goes out, follow him,' said Amelia, giving him a quick look. 'Of course, if it wasn't for harassing the Old Man, I would have insisted on going to the police. But he's – he's not *worldly*, Pat. You can't reason with him – at least, I can't. You will come, won't you?'

'All right,' agreed Dawlish. 'I'll come.'

Although he spoke reluctantly and almost gracelessly, the effect on Amelia was to make her spring to her feet in a single movement which was graceful beyond words. Reaching him, she bent down and brushed his forehead with her lips.

He prepared himself for an orgy of thanks, but after

10

squeezing his hand and saying: 'I *knew* you would,' Amelia stepped swiftly towards the house.

'Now I wonder who she's going to tell?' ruminated Dawlish as he watched her go.

Chapter 2

The Reputation of Dr Shortt

Without eagerness Dawlish followed in Amelia's wake. Crossing a sunlit stretch of lawn, his large figure, clad in casual grey flannels could not be better appreciated. Such a man might have been expected to walk cumbersomely, but Dawlish moved almost as gracefully and quite as swiftly as Amelia. He ran up the short flight of stone steps leading to the side entrance to Clay House, entered a subsidiary hall, and then reached the main one, a vast chamber beset with statues of modern design, grotesque and rather horrible, the walls adorned with equally hideous surrealist paintings.

A grey-haired maid was coming from the lounge.

'Have you seen Miss Shortt?' asked Dawlish.

'Someone just ran upstairs, sir,' said the maid. She smiled; most women smiled at Dawlish.

He heard a door close towards the right of the landing.

He mounted the stairs quickly and pushed the door open an inch. Almost immediately he heard the lifting of a telephone receiver, and presently Amelia's voice, which just carried to Dawlish's ears.

'Bing, darling, thank heavens, I thought you might be out. . . . Yes, he's fallen for it! . . . Absolutely, he was really very easy. . . . What? . . . Yes, exactly what we arranged. Of course I'm sure . . . yes, tonight. I'll get him there about ten o'clock, that ought to be all right. . . . *Yes*, darling, I do.' There was an appreciable pause, and then a light laugh. 'I shouldn't worry about that if I were you. I must go now, the door might open at any minute . . .'

The ting of the receiver being replaced and the faint sound of the door closing were simultaneous.

Dawlish sped along the passage, nipping behind a door marked 'Cloaks'.

It was several minutes before Amelia passed him heading for the stairs. From his vantage point he could see that her lovely eyes were very bright. She walked as a woman who was delighted with herself, the full skirt of her frock swirling triumphantly about her shapely legs.

Dawlish's lips curved, for he was amused in spite of the somewhat disparaging terms in which Amelia had discussed him. For a brief second he had contemplated walking in on her, but that temptation had quickly gone. For the time being it was better for Amelia to think him completely deceived.

He was puzzled as he made his way to his room, but too tired to give the matter much thought.

Not a man who tired easily, he had spent five days and nights in a small and airless room at Whitehall wrestling with problems which had confronted his particular segment of the British Intelligence Department. Now all he wanted was to rest.

Clay House had appeared the ideal spot for that. Sir Jeremy Clay, its owner, was a man of great wealth, his charming and attractive wife much given to good works. Out of the two things and the fact that the house was too large for them in time of war, had sprung the Services Leave Club. The mansion had been turned into a combination of hotel, hostel, and hospital – or more accurately conva-lescent home – where the only *visa* required was a uniform and a leave pass. The Leave Club was run on non-profit lines, no charge being made except for drinks: payment was left to the discretion of the guests.

Amelia, on leave from the W.A.A.F., had every right to be there. For that matter Dawlish's fiancée, Felicity, hoped to spend the Sunday there provided she could get away from the pressing duties of an A.T.S. unit in the Home Counties. Dawlish had considered it an ideal spot for his precious weekend; and thus it would have been but for the persistance of Amelia.

His room, a small one, overlooked a part of the garden. Tall trees shielded it from the Park beyond. The hum of traffic was very faint. Dawlish opened the window to its fullest, then stepped across to the door and locked it. Reasonably satisfied that there would be no further inter-ruptions until the evening, he took off his shoes and laid down on the bed. Within five minutes, he was asleep.

It was still broad daylight when he woke up.

13

Glancing at his watch, he exclaimed aloud: 'Ten to seven, by George!'

Dinner was an elastic meal at Clay House, and, taking things easily, Dawlish lingered over a hot bath and a cold shower. A brisk rub down invigorated him, and when he returned to his room he felt fresher than he had done for some days past. Dressing, his thoughts touched only lightly on the subject of Amelia. He wondered what Felicity would have to say about it, then shrugged the thought away; in all probability it would be over by Sunday, Amelia's problem melting away before a few inquiries.

The dining-room was half-empty. A dozen diners called or waved or smiled towards him before he took a window seat where there was room only for one. The waiter whispered that there was a half-bottle of Burgundy, and Dawlish said 'yes' with alacrity.

When he thought back over this interim period, the thing which impressed him most was that he relished every moment of the meal, the leisureliness of Clay House, the quiet efficiency of the service. That other things were happening at other places was an immutable fact, that some of them might be intimately connected with his own actions in the course of the next few weeks did not occur to him.

The first thing to disturb him, even mildly, was a note from Amelia, delivered by a waiter who explained that the note had been mislaid and should have been delivered to him much earlier. Dawlish waved the apologies aside, glanced at Amelia's careless writing, slit the envelope with the back of a knife, and read:

Pat, I did want to have dinner with you tonight, but I've had to go out unexpectedly. I'll ring you by half-past seven at the latest. Don't forget your promise, will you? A.

Frowning, Dawlish called the waiter and inquired whether there had been a telephone call for him; at half-past seven he had been finishing his bath, and might not have received the summons to the telephone. The waiter promised to inquire, and returned after five minutes with the assurance that there had been no telephone call for Major Dawlish since that morning.

Vaguely troubled, for it was not like Amelia to be unpunctual in such circumstances, he took a stroll in the garden, wondering what he should do first. It was obvious that

14

before he went to Shortt's house he needed to know a little more about the man.

He ran through the names of his acquaintances.

Shortt was a well-known man in medical research, and to him were due several outstanding discoveries on the treatment of hitherto incurable diseases. The most likely man to give him information, thought Dawlish, was Dr Abel Rister, but although Rister knew him well and in most ways was a reliable confidant, he was also a consultant pathologist to the people at Scotland Yard.

'And it might not be wise to make him curious,' mused Dawlish.

He kept within sight of the main door, half-expecting a summons to the telephone, but none came.

His uneasiness about Amelia's failure to telephone him deepened. It was half-past eight, and she would surely want to get in touch with him about her plans for the night. He set the fears aside, and ran through his list of medical acquaintances again. Finally he decided to have a word with Dr Grayling, a family doctor and a familiar of Dawlish's boyhood. He telephoned Grayling, and was lucky to find him in.

He arranged to meet him at Wigmore Street, giving precise instructions with the telephone operator at Clay House for any call to be transferred to Grayling's number. As he left the house, he looked about him for any indication of Amelia's return. There was none, nor was there a message for him when he reached Grayling's house, and was ushered into the doctor's first-floor study.

Grayling was a short, square man, sturdy of body and heavy of face. By nature gruff and abrupt, thirty odd years of a West End practice had softened him very little.

Dawlish thought he looked tired, but found no slackening in the firmness of his handclasp.

'I didn't think you could be ill,' said Grayling. 'A cigar?' Dawlish declined and took out his pipe, and Grayling followed his example. 'The only time you need a doctor is when you get knocked about. You haven't been in the limelight much lately, have you?'

'Happily, no,' agreed Dawlish.

'Happily?' Grayling raised his eyebrows. 'Don't try to bluff me, Patrick, I know that you revel in it.'

'It' summarised all the activities of Patrick Dawlish over

the past five years, during which he had figured in a number of sensational cases, building for himself a reputation which was almost legendary. One of Dawlish's complaints was that no one believed him when he declared that he did not embark upon the escapades from choice. It was true, however, that he had an almost uncanny way of being there when things happened. Sensing now that Grayling had little time to spare he came promptly to the point.

He did not imagine the change of expression on Grayling's face when Dr Shortt was mentioned.

The change, however, was difficult to define. There was nothing antagonistic in his attitude in any way, but there was a hint of diffidence. Dawlish would not have been surprised had Grayling followed this change of expression by touching his forehead with a meaning forefinger, and allowed him to draw his own conclusions.

He said repressively: 'Yes, I know Shortt fairly well, Patrick.'

'What's he like?' asked Dawlish bluntly.

'Like?' Grayling smiled. 'Like no one else, but you could say the same of many of the research men. A most likeable fellow with an absolute devotion to his work, but – well, let's be honest about this, and not beat about the bush. He's been overworking, and it's not doing him any good.'

'Mental fatigue, you mean?'

'It's as good a term as any, yes,' said Grayling.

'What are the symptoms?' asked Dawlish.

'They vary. In Shortt – I'm speaking in the strictest confidence, Patrick, but you know that – they manifest themselves mostly in unexpected aberrations from the normal. He will be in the middle of a discourse on, say, the modern methods of blood transfusion, and then he will start talking about his dog, or his daughter – anything, in fact, but the original subject. Then he gets back to it, but gives the impression that he doesn't know that he's made any digression. I saw him only three days ago, and the damnable thing is that there's no suggestion that he realises that he needs a rest.'

'Can't anyone tell him?' For the first time since reaching the Wigmore Street house Dawlish remembered Amelia, and glanced towards the telephone. It remained, however, silent.

Dawlish looked back at Grayling, who was answering:

'Several of us have tried, but he's a most difficult man to

approach. He's so deeply buried in his present research that he won't think of anything else until it's over.'

'Have you any idea what it's about?' asked Dawlish.

Grayling looked at him.

'Patrick, just why are you asking these questions?'

Dawlish drew a deep breath. He hesitated only for a moment before saying:

'His daughter told me a rather intriguing story, and I'm following it up at her urgent request – although not necessarily the way she expects.' His eyes twinkled.

'Oh,' said Grayling, patently surprised. 'I didn't think she ever thought of anything but herself. Featherbrained little – ' He paused abruptly, and smiled. 'But perhaps she's a friend of yours?'

'Not particularly,' said Dawlish, 'but my impression was a little different. Selfish, yes, but hardly featherbrained.'

'Use what word you like, it means the same,' growled Grayling. He smiled a little grimly, and then went on: 'You asked me what Shortt's buried in at the moment. I can't tell you in so many words, and I doubt whether anyone else can. But I can tell you one of its branches. He's just written an astonishing paper on the treatment of bomb-and-shell-shock.'

Dawlish nodded slowly.

'It's not a high percentage,' Grayling emphasised, 'but it affects a growing number of people. We aren't in possession of all the facts and figures, but there's no doubt that a new mental type – I'm speaking very simply,' he added with a quick smile, 'is springing up in the occupied countries still under German rule. They're not mad: they just have no interest in living or in doing anything. They're' – he searched for a word – 'mentally sterile.'

'Where does Shortt come in?'

'He's developing an entirely new treatment,' said Grayling. 'Nothing more nor less than – how shall I put this? – physical stimulation of the brain. An injection *into* the brain. It has worked, he claims on straightforward shell-shock cases, although it's in the experimental stage and no one can be sure that the effect will be lasting. You see what it means?'

Dawlish nodded.

'Well, I can't tell you much more than that, only that it's his main problem and preoccupation. He makes a discovery in the course of his researches and, if it offers any hope of development, concentrates on it for a while before coming back to what he started on. That's unusual, of course, but not remarkable.'

Dawlish pursed his lips.

'Perhaps not. There's an odd connection, though. He introduces subsidiary subjects into his general conversation today, you say?' Grayling nodded. 'That's a natural consequence of doing exactly the same thing in his researches. Then, he made a discovery which side-tracked him. Now, he has a thought which side-tracks him. Yes?'

Grayling looked at him in some surprise.

'Very aptly put.'

'The lay-mind sometimes sees the obvious even if it doesn't see what causes it,' Dawlish declared lightly. 'Shortt isn't what you'd call the most brilliant man in his field, is he?'

'No – although in that particular field he's almost alone,' said Grayling. 'He starts off brilliantly enough but his habit of leaving the main thing means that many people get there before him. I don't know of any man more respected for what he's done, but he never gets the cream.'

'Hm,' said Dawlish. 'Is he rich?'

Grayling considered.

'Well, I suppose so,' he said at last. 'He gets grants for most of his researches, but a man who can maintain his Jermyn Street house can't be exactly a pauper. And his daughter spends freely enough – too freely,' added Grayling, allowing his dislike of Amelia to prejudice his views. 'What on earth made you ask that?'

'Oh, just a general curiosity,' said Dawlish blandly. 'What kind of staff has he got, do you know?'

'I think he has two laboratory assistants,' said Grayling. 'He does the main work himself, he's not dependent on assistance to any marked degree, and when he wants a lot done he goes to one of the hospitals or universities. If you mean household staff, I've no idea at all. He can't have much, these days.'

'No,' admitted Dawlish. 'Well, you've been more than helpful, Doc. I was very much in the air before I came, and now I shall know something when Amelia tackles me again.' He put his hands on the arms of his chair, and rose quickly.

'It's always good to have a talk with you, Patrick. And –'

Grayling broke off, as the telephone bell shrilled out. He

18

lifted the receiver, and then, after a long pause, turned in surprise to Dawlish.

'It's for you.'

'Thanks,' said Dawlish, and took the telephone quickly.

Chapter 3

The Home of Dr Shortt

It was not Amelia. Dawlish felt a sharp sense of disappointment at the sound of an unfamiliar voice.

'Is that Major Dawlish?'

'Yes.'

'I have been asked to give you a message, Major Dawlish, by a friend of Miss Amelia Shortt's.'

Immediately Dawlish was on guard. He disliked the roundabout way in which this message was being presented. There was no assurance that Amelia had prompted it.

'Miss Shortt will not be able to keep her appointment with you for tonight,' the voice went on, 'because she has been involved in a slight accident. Not so serious, I was asked to assure you, as was feared at first, when her father was summoned.'

'Where is she now?'

'I am afraid I don't know, sir.' The voice, Dawlish noted, had a slight lisp. 'I had this message from a friend, and was asked to pass it on to you immediately. I have no more information for you. Goodbye, sir.'

'Just a moment!' exclaimed Dawlish. 'What is the name of Miss Shortt's friend?'

Dawlish heard the abrupt disconnection, and knew that it would be useless to attempt any further conversation. Frowning, he replaced the receiver and looked round to find Grayling eyeing him with no pretence at indifference.

'Bad news, Dawlish?'

'I wouldn't like to say,' said Dawlish slowly. 'Unexpected news, certainly. Do you happen to know Shortt's telephone number?'

'It will be on my pad,' said Grayling.

He opened a drawer in the desk, drew out an indexed pad, and ran through it. 'Mayfair 0132.'

'May I use the 'phone?' asked Dawlish, and immediately

began to dial. He was vaguely aware that Grayling was eyeing him with surprise and some concern, aware also that he must be creating a disturbing impression. He felt disturbed, for there had been a vagueness about that telephone message which he disliked.

After a long pause, while he heard the intermittent ringing of the telephone at Shortt's house, a quavering voice, obviously that of a very old man, asked:

'Who is that? Who is that? I can't hear very well, speak plainly please.'

'My name is Major Dawlish,' said Dawlish, enunciating the words carefully. 'And I would like to – '

'What did you say?' demanded the old man testily.

Dawlish began again.

'My name is Major Dawlish, and I would like to speak to – '

'Did you say Cornish? I can't hear very well. Who do you want? If it's Dr Shortt, he isn't at home, he won't be home tonight. Nor will Miss Shortt.'

Dawlish was frowning as he rang off.

'A message from a nameless friend, and a deaf butler,' he murmured. 'It's odd. Very odd.'

'I suppose you know what you're talking about,' said Grayling a little testily.

Dawlish beamed upon him.

'As a matter of fact, I don't. But there's no need to worry about it.'

'If I can help – ' began Grayling.

'I'll let you know,' Dawlish assured him. 'At the moment you've been more than useful.'

He left the house with renewed thanks, walking from it very thoughtfully. Two or three people passed along the pavement, but he was hardly aware of them. He was heedless, also, of what Grayling had told him. At that moment his interest was in effects rather than causes, and to him it seemed at least possible that Amelia had either:

(a) Met with an accident which had been deliberately contrived to draw her and her father from London and prevent Dawlish from visiting Jermyn Street.

(b) Made up the accident story as a way of discouraging his interest now that it had been aroused.

Those two things gave him plenty to think about, but there was a third possibility – that there had been no accident but that the message had been sent to him to make sure that he did not press his inquiries into the affair of Dr Shortt and his lovely daughter.

Completely gone now was Dawlish's reluctance to spend time on the affair. That was partly due to the revivifying effect of the afternoon sleep, and partly because the affair was developing very differently from what he had expected. Still brooding on it, he boarded a bus going to St John's Wood, near enough for him to walk to Clay House. By the time he had left the bus he had decided that theorising on what had happened would be unprofitable. He knew the superficial facts, and the time might come when he could put them into their proper order. For the moment he could only map out some kind of plan of campaign for himself.

He did not consciously think of going to Jermyn Street, but it did not occur to him to stay away. The quavering voice and the deaf man were alone intriguing. They might be genuine, but to Dawlish they looked surprisingly like a part of a well-directed plan to keep him in ignorance of what had happened.

It was dusk by then, and London was remarkably quiet, the grounds of Clay House blanketed by the surrounding noiselessness. The front door of the club was open, and Dawlish went up to the small lounge.

There were half-a-dozen people lolling in easy chairs, chatting or looking at the evening papers. Dawlish waved a hand in greeting, then stepped to the telephone. He dialled a Mayfair number, and for a long time there was no answer; then at last he heard the receiver being taken off. An irritable, sleepy voice answered him.

'Who the blazes are you? I – good gad! Pat? I call it downright disgraceful,' declared Beresford with feeling. 'For five days and nights I work until my eyes nearly fall out of my head, and when I do get a few minutes for sleep you wake me up. The devil take you. What's the matter?'

'I don't know yet,' said Dawlish, 'but I'll be round in twenty minutes, and I want you to be up and ready for a walk.'

'Walk!' cried Beresford, his voice cracking in dismay. 'Look here, old man, you're not serious? You don't really want me to get up?' His voice cracked again. 'Confound it, I –'

'It's urgent,' said Dawlish firmly. 'I'll be round in twenty minutes.'

'But – ' began Beresford on a high note.

'Twenty minutes,' repeated Dawlish, and rang off.

He turned and contemplated the people in the easy chairs. One of them, a bearded naval officer, got up unobtrusively and followed him.

As Dawlish reached his own room, a voice called from the passage:

'Dawlish – can you spare a minute?'

'Just about,' said Dawlish. 'What is it?' He knew the voice to be that of Hubbard, a name not unfamiliar in the annals of submarine warfare.

'I – er – ' began Hubbard.

Dawlish smiled on him drily.

'I know,' he said. 'You heard me talking to Ted Beresford and you wondered if there was anything brewing. You crave a spot of brightness in the pall of London. The answer is – '

Hubbard laughed, then added hastily: 'Think before you say "no", old chap. I can be quite useful at times. Fact.' He looked anxious and hopeful. 'I mean, you were moaning this afternoon about not getting any sleep in a fortnight, and that you and Beresford were going to sleep the clock round. And here you are, all bright and merry, dragging the poor fellow out of bed. I mean, something's up, isn't it?'

Dawlish smiled.

'Well, you must admit it's queer,' Hubbard went on. 'And if anything is brewing in your line, I might come in useful. I'm here for a week,' he added guilefully, 'and I've nothing much to do. Why don't you let Beresford stay in bed, and use me?'

Dawlish chuckled.

'Not now. Ted wouldn't miss anything for a pension.'

'So there *is* something up,' declared Hubbard triumphantly.

'I wouldn't go any further than to say there might be,' Dawlish assured him, 'but if you're really longing for a scrap, come along. No promises,' he added warningly.

'Oh, good man!' exclaimed Hubbard,

Dawlish looked at him, not sure whether he had been wise in bowing to the other's pleading. It was too early in the affair to be sure that any investigation was really needed, and yet it did not occur to him to sit back and allow things to

take their course. Instead, he took from an attaché case a
.32 automatic. His post at Whitehall made it legal for him
to carry a loaded gun, and he preferred to have the means at
hand for both defensive and offensive action.

Hubbard widened his eyes, which were youthful and
brown.

'Like that, is it?'

'You get wet if you don't carry a mackintosh,' Dawlish
said cheerfully, 'but it rarely rains if you do. Are you ready?'

Some fifteen minutes later they walked up the steps of the
Brook Street flat where Ted Beresford was staying. The flat
was a communal one, shared by Beresford, Dawlish, another
of their kind named Jeremy, as well as by Felicity Deverall
and a friend in the A.T.S. For a flat with four rooms that
was a crowd; in actual fact there were rarely more than three
of them occupying it at the same time, and it solved their
leave problem well enough.

Beresford, an ugly man with an ugliness that was both
homely and endearing, opened the door with some eagerness. In stature he was as big, if not bigger, than Dawlish,
and together, they filled the hall.

He contrived the nearly impossible, by smiling at Hubbard
and scowling at Dawlish.

'If you haven't a very good reason for yanking me out of
bed, I'm going back to it,' he declared.

Dawlish led the way to the small lounge of the flat, while
Beresford brought two bottles of ale from a cabinet, and
proceeded to fill three tankards.

As they drank, Dawlish gave a brief résumé of what had
happened. At the end of it Beresford accepted the decision
to go to Jermyn Street with equanimity.

'Is there any point in going, if they're both away?'
Hubbard asked.

Beresford chuckled.

'A *very* young disciple,' he said. 'If Amelia was expecting
Shortt to meet someone, and Shortt doesn't turn up, the
second party might go to Mohammed – if you see what I
mean.'

A little more than fifteen minutes later Dawlish rang the
bell at 22g Jermyn Street, having explained on the way that
the first thing necessary was to find what the interior of the
house was like, and to get an impression of the servants. All
three of them waited in the porch while the echoes of the bell

24

faded. After a long pause Dawlish rang again. There was no answer; nor was there any response when Dawlish lifted the knocker, bringing it down with a bang.

'You said he was deaf,' whispered Beresford.

'Surely there's someone here who can hear,' protested Hubbard.

'That's the spirit,' agreed Dawlish. 'Always assume the probable, but be prepared for the opposite. The thing is, what to do? Supposing we try the back entrance,' he added. 'It might be nearer the servants' and yield better results.'

To get to the back of 22g Jermyn Street it was necessary to walk as far as a narrow by-road which bisected it, and then to walk along a service alley. Doors leading to the gardens were marked in white, and they were able to find 22g by the light of Dawlish's torch. The more furtive element in the rear approach clearly satisfied Hubbard's longing for excitement; Dawlish noticed with amusement that he walked on tiptoe.

The doorway into the narrow garden was not locked.

'*Open sesame,*' murmured Dawlish, and led the way to the house along a narrow, paved path.

The beam of his torch fixed at a higher level, Dawlish kicked against something which did not move, and yet yielded to the toe of his shoe. It sent him lurching forward. Recovering, Dawlish shone his torch downwards.

'What is it?' demanded Hubbard.

He did not need a spoken answer, for the light shone on a man's face, dead white in the glare. The eyes were open and peered sightlessly upward, the lips were parted. In no way was it a pleasant sight, but all of them were conversant with death.

'Proof of the pudding, Pat.'

'Yes,' admitted Dawlish, 'but another question, too. Why bring him out here?'

Chapter 4

Why, Indeed

Hubbard said stoutly: 'Well, he's here, and that's what we have to worry about. I suppose – ' The sailor hesitated.

'What do you suppose?' asked Dawlish.

'That he was murdered.'

'It looks like it,' said Dawlish cautiously. 'He's certainly dead, but it's a queer place for a man to die. If it were daylight we'd be able to see better, but if it were daylight he probably wouldn't be here.' Thus speaking, Dawlish went down on one knee, shining his torch more fully into the dead man's face. For formality's sake he felt his pulse, but the hand was already cold.

'Try the door, Ted,' said Dawlish absently.

He slipped his hand into the dead man's breast pocket as he spoke, then withdrew it, empty. The other large pockets yielded nothing at all, but Ted's mission of discovery did, for he spoke with a tinge of excitement in his voice.

'It's unlocked.'

'Good,' said Dawlish, straightening up. 'Come on, Hubbard.'

'But aren't you going to take him inside?' demanded Hubbard, looking at the solitary figure on the ground, the pallid face now no more than a blur, for the beam of light had shifted.

'I am not,' said Dawlish emphatically. 'He stays there until the police arrive.'

'Police?' echoed Hubbard, aghast. 'But I thought – '

'You probably thought that I considered myself above all police rules and regulations and the law of the common man,' suggested Dawlish. 'I'm not – that is, not always,' he added with a ghost of a chuckle. 'Nothing that's happened here needs immediate attention, and the wise thing is to annoy the police only when there's nothing else to be done.'

'But I thought you – er – you were more or less one of

them,' said Hubbard, still dazedly.

'An occasional consultant, no more,' said Dawlish. 'What we can do is to look through the house.' He gripped Hubbard's arm firmly and led him in Ted's wake, inside a kitchen of some proportions. Except for a quick glance about him Dawlish showed no interest in it, nor in the long, narrow passage which ended in a short flight of steps, and a door. The door led into the main hall of 22g Jermyn Street.

The only light was the one which Ted had switched on in the passage. Too far away to be of much help, its dimmed radiance seemed only to cast shadows all about them, making the silence seem even more profound, more eerie. Glancing upward, the staircase appeared to go on and on, without end; they could see its wooden bannisters and polished balustrade curving at the landings, disappearing into deep pockets of darkness.

Nothing indicated that there was anyone about the house. Dawlish, moving slowly and thoughtfully, found the main light switch and pressed it down, flooding the hall with sudden, blinding brilliance.

'Now we'll start,' said Dawlish. 'Ted, stay in the hall while Hubbard and I look through the downstairs rooms.' He ushered Hubbard into the nearest, a long narrow dining-room empty of people. To make sure he walked round it, peering in the corners and behind furniture, but there was no one there.

The other ground floor reception rooms were smaller, but all were equally deserted.

'No go,' said Dawlish briefly.

The three of them went to the first floor. Dawlish led the way, but found nothing of interest; the main room was an enormous lounge, but that too, like the dining room, emitted the slightly musty odour of a room infrequently used. The other rooms, one a comfortable sitting room, the other a library, were more cheerful, but equally empty.

'No sign of violence here,' murmured Dawlish.

On the second floor were five bedrooms, all empty of people and all but one showing no signs of recent occupation. That one contained cosmetics in profusion, and a dusting of powder which suggested that Amelia had used it fairly recently. A faint perfume lingered in the air of the room, while a flimsy nightdress was lying carelessly across the bed.

'Now, now,' murmured Dawlish, as he led Hubbard out.

The eeriness was no longer imaginary; it was felt by them all, that strange atmosphere of a house so recently occupied – for Dawlish assumed that Dr Shortt had lived there – and now empty of life. But on the next floor, there was a change. They came upon a small study, so crammed with books and furniture that there was just enough room for the three of them to stand. The desk was littered with papers; a shorthand notebook rested against a typewriter.

There were cigarette butts in an ashtray.

From the room abutted one which was evidently a laboratory. Along one wall, beneath heavily curtained windows, was a bench littered with such miscellany of instruments, glassware and the general impedimenta of research that it beggared description. A skeleton dangled from a piece of wire suspended from the ceiling, its shadow grotesque against white distemper. There were two desks, one of them covered with papers and a pencil. The lead of the pencil was broken, and beneath it a scrawled mark on paper suggested that it had broken while in use.

'A sudden interruption, I wonder?' mused Dawlish.

He looked searchingly at the floor.

'Got any ideas?' queried Beresford.

'I don't know,' said Dawlish. He went down on one knee behind the desk where the pencil had broken. 'This has been washed recently, there are wet patches.' His fingers ran lightly over the surface. 'Ah! – a dark brown spot the size of a sixpence,' he added cheerfully. 'Could it be blood? Clue for the sleuth here, I fancy.'

'But aren't you – ' Hubbard began, eying the little spot eagerly. 'I mean, I thought – '

'You see how you overestimated me,' murmured Dawlish. 'If I do anything at all in these things I do it by blind luck.'

'Says he,' said Beresford. 'Is that all, Pat?'

'I can't see much else,' admitted Dawlish, 'and – hallo, what's that?'

A sound wafted up from the well of the stairs. It was a sharp tapping sound, but, because of the height of the house, it seemed distant. After a pause it was repeated.

'Three, four, knock at the door,' Dawlish said lightly. 'Some unfortunate is trying to get in.'

'Do you think – ' began Hubbard, and then stopped short, flushing a little.

Dawlish grinned.

28

'I think the two of you had better stay here. I'll see who it is, and if I whistle, you come down.'

'One day you will take too much on yourself and get hit over the head,' Beresford warned him. And to Hubbard: 'The tyke always takes the limelight if there's half a chance, all we have to do is stand aside and say "yes sir" and "no sir".' He smiled genially.

Dawlish reached the first-floor landing in time to hear a bell ringing long and insistently. Whoever was there certainly meant to advertise their presence. He did not hesitate when he reached the hall, but put his left hand in his pocket, where he kept the automatic.

In spite of his casualness upstairs, he was not unaffected by the eerie atmosphere of the house. Except for the table in the laboratory, and the traces of occupation in Amelia's room, its emptiness held a strange quality. Even in time of war such a house, especially when tenanted by a man whose work was quite certainly of high national importance, should have had several servants. There was no sign of the doctor's two laboratory assistants, only that cold, pallid figure outside.

Dawlish wrenched open the door. Two uniformed men confronted him, and behind them he could see a stationary car.

Well, well, thought Dawlish, if it isn't the police.

'Is this the home of Dr Shortt?'

'To the best of my knowledge, yes,' said Dawlish courteously.

The men stepped swiftly into the hall. They were about him in a second, hemming him in on all sides although doing nothing ostentatious enough to suggest that he was being harassed. There were five in all, three in uniform and two plainclothes men.

One of the latter looked levelly at Dawlish.

'Did you telephone Scotland Yard?' he demanded.

'Certainly not,' Dawlish assured him. So someone had telephoned the Yard. It gave rise to further complications but he did not let thought of them sink in, for the C.I.D. man was regarding him even more searchingly.

'And you're not sure whether this is Dr Shortt's house?'

'Reasonably sure.'

'I'll be glad if you'll stay here while I have a look round,' said the Yard man briskly, and then, as if he remembered a formality which he had not complied with, turned back. 'What right have you to be here?'

'None at all,' admitted Dawlish. 'What right have you?'

'I am an officer of the law –' the man began.

'Well, perhaps,' said Dawlish. 'Can I see your authority – and your search warrant?'

Rather stiffly Detective Sergeant William Glee complied. 'And who are you, please?'

Dawlish took out his wallet. He extracted a card which was signed by his immediate Chief, Colonel Whitehead, and countersigned by a distant relative of Dawlish's, the Chief Commissioner at Scotland Yard.

Glee looked at it, casually at first, and then his eyes scanned the large man's face with sharp interest.

'*That* Dawlish!' he exclaimed. 'Why –'

Without more preamble Dawlish told him of the body outside, his search, and even his discoveries, minor though they were. He skated skilfully over the reason for his visit, eliciting from Glee the fact that someone had telephoned the Yard crying murder and worse; but the caller had not given a name or telephone number, and it had been some time before the call had been traced to 22g Jermyn Street.

By then they were in the kitchen.

A fancy, no more, flashed through Dawlish's mind: supposing the body had been removed? He confounded himself for not leaving Ted or Hubbard to look after it. But it was there, stark in the light of a bull's eye lantern.

Glee put the investigation in hand with quick, quiet efficiency.

He gave little information about what was found in the dead man's pockets, was friendly enough, but when he had finished suggested that Dawlish might like to accompany him to the Yard.

It was nearly half-past eleven when they left. On the pavement outside Number 22g Hubbard and Beresford stood watching the red rear-lamp disappear from sight. The sound of the car engine faded, and quiet descended upon the centre of London.

Hubbard drew a deep breath.

'I'd never have believed it!'

'Believed what?' asked Ted Beresford mildly.

'Dawlish. I thought he –' Hubbard paused. 'I mean, I took it for granted that he would know exactly what to do,

and that he'd have no truck with the Roberts. He seemed' –
he paused, searching for a word – 'he seemed, well, *disinterested*. I'm beginning to think you're right, others do the
work and Dawlish gets the reputation.'

Beresford put a large hand on the sailor's shoulder.

'Men,' he declared deeply, 'were deceivers ever, but none
so deeply as Dawlish. Don't worry about him, Hub, he's
getting the thing worked out in his mind.' They started to
walk towards Brook Street. 'What do you suggest he could
have done?'

'Well, I don't know,' said Hubbard spiritedly. 'All I know
is that I expected him to do *something*.'

'In due course he will,' said Beresford, 'and I don't think
we'll get much sleep tonight. Not if I know that look in his
eye. Will you come to the flat? He'll turn up there when he's
through at the Yard, and be ready for a pow-wow.'

'Is there room?' asked Hubbard, eagerly.

'Just about.'

They reached Brook Street and strolled towards the house
where Dawlish and Beresford had the flat. It was very quiet
and the sky was filled with stars. There was a dim blue light
burning halfway up the stairs so that they could just see
their way.

Inside the flat, Beresford switched the light on and was
the first to see the little envelope tucked beneath the door.
It was printed: 'Telegram', and on it was Dawlish's name and
the address of the flat. Beresford hesitated, then slit open the
envelope. The message was brief and to the point.

*Need your help desperately stop can you drop everything
and come to 81 Mere Street, Manchester stop can't
possibly manage London this weekend stop do try darling
Felicity.*

Reading it over Beresford's shoulder, Hubbard said:
'Who's Felicity?'

'Felicity Deverall,' said Beresford gently, 'is Dawlish's
fiancee.' He stepped towards the telephone and began to
dial Whitehall 1212. 'The quicker Pat knows about this the
better.'

'Do you mean he might drop everything and go away?'
demanded Hubbard in a high-pitched voice.

'This isn't from Felicity,' said Beresford briefly. 'She
wouldn't wire, she'd 'phone. Wires aren't delivered after

31

half-past nine these days, anyhow, and this wasn't here when we left. Besides, she knows that Pat would normally be at Clay House.' He turned away from Hubbard and said into the telephone: 'Scotland Yard? . . . I think Major Dawlish is there, will you put me through, please?'

Chapter 5

Superintendent Trivett

Dawlish was well aware that Detective Sergeant Glee was puzzled by the presence of the three men at Jermyn Street, and not fully satisfied by Dawlish's account of his reason for being there. Consequently he was not surprised when he was left in the waiting room, while Glee went to make a verbal report.

He did not know, but would have been only mildly surprised had he done so, that with Inspector Wilder in the Chief Inspector's office was Superintendent Trivett, good-looking, well-dressed, and, at forty, the youngest Superintendent at the Yard.

He knew Dawlish well.

'He told me that he had been telephoned by Dr Shortt's daughter, and asked to visit the house,' said Glee. 'He didn't explain why he went round to the back when there was no answer, and why he looked through the place after finding the body, instead of ringing us up. Under the circumstances I thought I'd better ask him to come here, sir.'

Trivett nodded, smiling a little absently.

'Quite right, Glee. It's never wise to take Dawlish too much for granted. I'll see him myself,' he added, 'and send for you if there's anything that wants clearing up. Nothing else you want me for, Inspector?'

'No thanks,' said Wilder gruffly.

Trivett knew quite well that Wilder, his senior by twelve years, resented his higher position and the fact that he had taken over the case without giving him, Wilder, a chance to get his teeth into it. Wilder was one of the trials of the Yard. Trivett did not give him much thought, however, when he reached his own small office and telephoned for Dawlish to be sent up.

When the big man appeared, Trivett pushed a box of cigarettes across the desk towards him.

'Now what have you been up to?'

'Delving after secrets,' said Dawlish. 'Thanks. How are you Bill? You look a bit tired.'

Trivett shrugged.

'Who doesn't?' He stifled a yawn. His eyes were faintly red at the rims, and lacked their usual brightness. 'Tired isn't the word for it,' he added. 'We're feeling the effect of the pressure, I suppose. Thank the Lord the war isn't likely to last all that much longer, and we'll be able to take it easier. But that isn't what I wanted to talk about. Why go to Jermyn Street, Pat?'

'Didn't Glee believe me?'

'He wasn't altogether convinced.'

Dawlish chuckled.

'A likely man, you ought to make a lot of him, Bill. It's true enough as far as it goes, although Amelia Shortt didn't ask me to go by telephone, she arranged it in person. And she was going to meet me at the house – Clay House, where I'm staying – to take me to Jermyn Street tonight. She was worried, she said, about her father, whom she was convinced was being blackmailed.'

Trivett, his eyes keener now, nodded.

'That's about all there is to it,' Dawlish assured him. 'Except that I had a message telling me that she had been involved in a slight accident, and also that her father had been summoned to her side. A deliberate stall, I thought, by someone who wanted to head me off. I thought I'd better have a look round.'

'I see,' said Trivett, and stretched out his hand to press a bell-push. 'What else haven't you told me?'

'Nothing of consequence,' Dawlish said mildly.

'No? This is a private business, Pat. There's murder in it. You won't take a lot on yourself, will you?'

Dawlish chuckled again.

'Dark warning by dutiful policeman! Actually Amelia wasn't keen on the police knowing. She was worried because Shortt had been sleeping badly, and was afraid of what you people might discover, I think. I didn't propose to let her down, and did all I could before you came along.'

'If we hadn't had the call, you'd probably have gone through the house thoroughly and left us the pickings,' Trivett said, a little severely. He looked up as Sergeant Glee appeared. 'Oh, Glee, find out if there's any report of an accident today to Miss Amelia Shortt, will you? Dr Shortt's daughter. And let me know as quickly as you can.'

'No wonder the police always get their man,' said Dawlish admiringly. 'What a system!'

'If we depended on blind luck and hunches, like some people, the criminal class would be the most affluent in England,' said Trivett, a little smugly. 'Did you take anything out of Kibb's pockets?'

'Kibb's?'

'The dead man at Jermyn Street.'

'No, there was nothing in any of the pockets where I looked. So you've got him labelled, have you?' Dawlish looked his curiosity, but did not put it into words. Trivett hesitated, and then went some measure towards satisfying it.

'He's Thomas Kibb, an old servant of Dr Shortt's. I think it was he who telephoned us, and that he was killed before he could finish the message. And I further think,' added Trivett, 'that he was being taken away when you arrived at the front door, and whoever wanted him off the premises left in a hurry, thinking you were the police. Does that satisfy you?'

'It seems reasonable enough to me,' admitted Dawlish. 'You wouldn't know if he was deaf, would you?'

Trivett's forehead wrinkled in surprise.

'He was, yes. There was one of those battery sets in his room. How did you know?'

Dawlish told him, and then said slowly: 'On the whole, it doesn't look too good, Bill. What do you know of Shortt? Anything outstanding?'

'I know little or nothing at the moment,' said Trivett, 'but I hope to get information before the morning. I – Yes? Come in.'

A tap at the door heralded Glee. There had been no report at all of any accident to Miss Amelia Shortt in the London area, he said. Should he get in touch with the Home Counties police? Trivett said 'yes', watched Glee depart, then stifled another yawn.

'Why do things have to happen at night?' wondered Dawlish. 'Is there anything else you want me for, Bill?'

Trivett said slowly: 'I don't think so. But before you go –' He hesitated, smiling a little. 'I needn't rub it in, Pat, but you aren't officially in this, you know. Don't trade on your card of authority too much, will you?'

'In other words, will I be a good boy and report everything to the police?' said Dawlish lightly. 'If I really had my way, Bill, I'd spend the whole of tomorrow in bed, and Sunday asleep in the garden. But I'm worried about Amelia, and she has shown a more touching faith in me than the police have done.'

Deliberately he said nothing of Amelia's deception: for the time being he considered that it was wiser to keep that to himself. He needed no telling that Trivett was aware of certain mental reservations, but the Superintendent did not say so, and Dawlish was on his feet when the telephone rang. It did not occur to him that he was wanted, and he was at the door when Trivett looked up and said quickly:

'For you, Pat.'

'Oh,' said Dawlish. 'Thanks.' He reached the desk and took the telephone from Trivett's hand, conscious of the deliberate gaze of the other man. He listened, his face gradually hardening. 'Yes,' he said once, and again: 'Yes, of course. Well, it doesn't seem to be urgent. Ring Fel, will you, just to make sure. I'll be over before long.'

He replaced the receiver, looking at Trivett without apparently seeing him. Trivett fought a losing battle and was finally constrained to ask:

'Why ring Felicity?'

Dawlish said absently: 'Someone appears to have sent a telegram under her name, asking me to go up north. Only he or she sent it to the wrong address, and forgot that telegrams aren't delivered after six o'clock.' He paused, then added: 'Sorry if I seem a bit pre-occupied, Bill, but I can't see why they should take it for granted that I would hare up north without making sure it's not a ruse to get me away. Do they think I, or anyone else of normal intelligence, would drop everything and dash off because a wire's signed "Felicity"?'

'They shouldn't,' admitted Trivett.

'It isn't reasonable, Bill, although all the rest is understandable enough. Even the murder of Kibb – you did say Kibb?'

'Thomas Kibb, yes,' said Trivett.

'Odd name,' commented Dawlish. 'There's an explanation for all of it, even Kibb's murder and the hurried exit, if one assumes that Shortt is in trouble. But the mysterious "they" haven't been *fools* up to now. Not, that is, until they sent

36

that phoney telegram. It doesn't fit in with the general level of intelligence.' He paused, and eyed Trivett evenly. 'Do you agree?'

'You have an astonishing habit of seeing the weak spot,' admitted Trivett with almost reluctant admiration. 'I suppose you're driving at the possibility that they knew you'd realise it was a fake?'

'I am,' said Dawlish.

'Then why send it?' demanded Trivett.

'That's the question,' admitted Dawlish. 'I suppose there's just a chance, a faint one, that something's amiss with Felicity. I wonder. If they want to switch my attention from Amelia and her father to Felicity they've succeeded, but if they want to keep it there they must have a reason. I hope –' He paused. 'Bill, you've more weight than I have. Ring her unit, will you? Ask her C.O. to make sure that she isn't allowed to leave the camp on any pretext at all. Because if Felicity has had such a wire from me she might not take the precautions that I have. Bedford 81A18,' he added, and pushed the receiver into Trivett's hands.

Trivett was about to speak when the operator said:

'There's a call for you, sir. Will you take it first?'

'Who is it?' asked Trivett.

'I'll inquire, sir.' There was a pause, and then the operator went on in a voice which reflected some annoyance: 'It isn't really for you, it's for Major Dawlish, from a Captain Beresford.'

'Put him through,' said Trivett quickly, and passed the receiver back to Dawlish.

Dawlish's expression gave nothing away for the first few seconds, but then he began to smile, and finally he chuckled and said:

'Bless her heart!'

Trivett's curiosity was self-evident when Dawlish replaced the receiver, but the large man was in so good a temper that several seconds passed before he condescended to explain.

'Felicity rang the flat,' he said. 'I didn't do her justice, bless her. She had a wire earlier this evening to go to 81, Mere Street, Manchester – the same address as that on my wire, you'll remember – and signed by me. But she was out when it arrived. So as soon as she returned she telephoned Clay House, but although I wasn't there she still felt dissatisfied and rang through to the flat. Not bad, Bill.'

'No,' said Trivett slowly, but his hesitation was no reflection on the good sense of Felicity. 'Did you say the same address?'

'I did. Now it's getting clearer, and the intelligence level is rated high,' said Dawlish. 'Supposing she'd had the wire when it first arrived? Supposing she'd 'phoned me and been told that I'd left Clay House, which I would have done but for this and that? She would have gone haring up to Manchester, and of course left the Mere Street address. And I, telephoning the unit and finding she'd left it, wouid have assumed that the telegram was genuine and followed in her footsteps. Not bad at all,' added Dawlish with relish.

'It's too clever for my liking,' said Trivett gloomily.

'Clever, but not *too* clever,' amended Dawlish heartily. 'Those who planned it wouldn't go to much lengths to get me out of London and away from the Shortts unless they were afraid I might spoil something for them. So. the said something is of importance. Reasonable inference?' he demanded.

'Ye-es,' Trivett admitted grudgingly, and drew a deep breath. 'Why in the world something always happens to you I don't know. You don't look for the things, they come to you.'

'That's the first time I've ever heard you admit it,' said Dawlish, with satisfaction. 'I'm going to hold you to it. You know, Bill, I'm beginning to like this business.'

'Kibb was murdered,' Trivett said abruptly. 'Or didn't I tell you?'

'You probably did, but you didn't go into details. How?'

Trivett said blandly: 'By a knife in the back. Pat, this is essentially a police affair, and you've no need to interfere. We can look after Amelia Shortt and her father. Don't get yourself into trouble, because that's what it will mean unless you go off-stage right now.'

'Threat?' murmured Dawlish.

'Caution,' corrected Trivett.

'Noted,' said Dawlish, smiling lazily. 'I'll be good, Bill, unless, of course, the circumstances get too much for me.'

Trivett also smiled.

'While you've been busy,' he said, 'many things have happened. Amongst them your third cousin, or whatever relation Sir Archibald is to you, refused to lay up with a heavy cold and now has pneumonia. He'll be away for a month.'

'Oh,' said Dawlish, a little blankly.

It was not true that he traded on his distant relationship to Sir Archibald Morely, the Assistant Commissioner, but it was true that Morely allowed him to get away with more than he might have done had they been unrelated. Of late when Dawlish had been stirred to effort he had worked with the support of the Intelligence Department and the police had not had the authority to say 'yea' or 'nay', but it remained a fact that his association with Morely and with Trivett had been cohesive, even if he had not always met with approval. From Trivett's words he gathered that whoever was *locum tenens* in Morely's office was not likely to be at all amenable. Trivett would not say so in as many words, but his meaning was clear enough.

'Who's subbing for him?' asked Dawlish.

'Sir Lester Bray.'

Dawlish winced.

'Is he, by George. That does seem to hint at circumspection on my part. Nevertheless, you will ring Felicity's C.O. for me, won't you, and make sure that nothing goes wrong up there? I'll get Ted to slip up tomorrow and travel down with her. I can take defensive measures, I hope,' he added gently.

'I'll ring through,' promised Trivett.

Thoughtfully, Dawlish left Scotland Yard and walked towards Brook Street, keeping an eye open for a late taxi. He was preoccupied with the fact that Sir Lester Bray, for whom he had no regard at all, was Trivett's immediate superior for the time being. From Bray, his thoughts switched to the surprising fact that someone, presumably Amelia's 'friends', had gone to such length to get him away from London. Why?

He found neither an answer nor a taxi on his way back to Brook Street. He went upstairs leisurely, debating with himself how much to tell Hubbard, even wondering whether he had been wise to allow Hubbard to take any part in it. Unlike himself and Beresford, the sailor was a newcomer to any kind of work which might bring him in contact with the police. It would not be above Bray to make it extremely hot for Hubbard at the Admiralty.

Dawlish opened the door of the flat, and stepped into a

small hall. Voices came clearly to him, one of them only recently familiar.

'I tell you I must – must see him. I don't care what you say, it's essential.'

'Well, well,' mused Dawlish. 'The chappie with a lisp. This *is* progress.'

Chapter 6

The Man With The Lisp

Cautiously Dawlish turned the handle of the inner door and opened it an inch or two. He could just see the back of a plump man in dark clothes. The plumpness was made evident by a little ridge of fat below a shock of fair, curly hair. Neither Hubbard nor Beresford glanced at the door, yet Beresford, without a hairsbreadth change of countenance, would know it had been opened.

This was the difference between the two men; between Beresford, who knew Dawlish well and was not unfamiliar with affairs of violence and mystery, and Hubbard. For Hubbard would certainly have given himself away. As it was, the plump man, entirely unaware of Dawlish's imminence, continued to talk in his rather high-pitched, lisping voice.

'I don't care if I have to stay here all night,' he declared, 'I am going to see Dawlish. It's no use trying to put me off.'

'No one's trying to put you off,' said Beresford lightly.

'Yes you are. At all events you're trying to make me tell you what I want with Dawlish, but I shall tell no one, it is a matter for his ears alone. Now, be good enough to advise me when you expect him back.'

After a brief pause, Dawlish said: 'About now, I should think.'

The man with the lisp jumped inches from his chair as Dawlish advanced.

'Are – are you Dawlish? I didn't hear you come in.'

'Nor did I,' said Hubbard, his astonishment only slightly less than that of the other man's. 'How –'

'Does it matter how I came in?' asked Dawlish amiably. 'What about a drink, Ted, we aren't being hospitable to Mr. –' He paused, inquiringly.

'My name,' began the stranger, as his gaze hesitated between Dawlish and Beresford, who was getting beer from a cupboard nearby, 'is Bingham, Claude Bingham. You *are* Dawlish, aren't you?'

41

'Certainly I am,' said Dawlish perfunctorily.

Bingham drew a deep breath, preparatory to launching a portentous broadside. In most matters, Dawlish imagined, he would be portentous, but it was of little consequence. It was the name that mattered, for surely 'Bing' was the man who had talked to Amelia on the telephone. If Dawlish were right, another minor mystery was solved.

'Major Dawlish, I have something of extreme importance to say to you,' declared Bingham. 'It is a matter for your ears alone, and – '

Beresford thrust a foaming tankard in front of the plump man's face.

Bingham started, wrinkled his nose in distaste, and pushed the tankard away from him with no little violence.

'I do not drink alcohol. Major Dawlish – '

'*What?*' gasped Beresford, goggle-eyed.

'Will you kindly cease introducing irrelevant subjects?' demanded Bingham testily. 'Major Dawlish, this is a matter of considerable importance, and there is very little time to spare. Will you be good enough to allow me a few minutes in private consultation with you?'

Dawlish weighed the situation up quickly and came to the conclusion that Bingham would not talk freely in the presence of the others.

'This way, Mr Bingham,' he said stolidly.

Bingham bounded after him. The door of the small dining-room had barely shut before he declaimed in ringing tones:

'Major Dawlish, I am desperately in need of your help!'

'What about?' asked Dawlish practically.

'Before I discuss the subject matter,' cried Bingham dramatically, 'I must arrange the terms and conditions. I understand that you are not connected with the police or with Scotland Yard, but that you are able to undertake commissions of a strictly private nature, disclosing nothing of them to anyone, anyone at all. Is that so?'

Dawlish hesitated to say 'no' outright; the need for hearing Bingham's story, and the explanation of his undoubted agitation, being of primary importance.

Bingham obviously read something very different in his hesitation, for he struck another gesture and took out a wallet. From this he extracted a cheque book, and waved it temptingly before Dawlish's astonished eyes.

'Expense does not matter!' declared Bingham roundly.

42

'You may name your own figure, Major Dawlish, I shall not raise objections.'

Dawlish was on the point of saying that he was not a professional inquiry agent, but he stopped himself in time.

'My fees are high, Mr Bingham,' he said primly. 'I should want five thousand pounds.'

'F-five *thousand*!' gasped Bingham. 'It – but – I – '

'You did say that expense doesn't matter,' Dawlish reminded him blandly.

'Yes. Yes indeed. But five thousand – ' Bingham gulped. 'The figure seems excessive, Major Dawlish, you will admit that.'

'Perhaps,' said Dawlish.

'Can I – can I ask you to reconsider?' demanded Bingham.

'No,' said Dawlish uncompromisingly.

Bingham stared at him for several seconds, his full lips slightly parted. Dawlish remained expressionless, feeling quite sure that Bingham would begin to plead for more reasonable terms. But he was astonished in turn, for Bingham suddenly spoke with decision.

'Very well. But you can hardly expect all of it in advance. Shall we say one thousand pounds now, and the balance when the matter is satisfactorily concluded?'

For a moment Dawlish was bereft of speech.

He had established the fact that what Bingham was doing was worth five thousand pounds to whoever had sent him on this visit. There was at least a possibility that Amelia was connected with it. A man who was prepared to pay five thousand pounds for secret help – secret was the operative word, he knew – wanted that help very badly indeed.

But it had gone far enough, and he spoke thoughtfully.

'Sit down, Bingham. I think it's time you understood my position.' Bingham took a chair and Dawlish looked down on him, ignoring the cheque book. 'In the first place I don't need nor take money for helping anyone. Whether I help – if help's the word – or not, depends on whether I feel inclined.'

'But – but you said – ' began Bingham aghast.

'Enough to discover that you want help so badly that you'll pay an absurd sum for it,' Dawlish said gently.

Bingham stared at him. It crossed his mind, and Dawlish could almost see the path of it, that he had been lured into making a declaration without getting any guarantee of

Dawlish's discretion. The man was troubled; he swallowed hard once or twice, and brushed the over-long hair back from his forehead.

Dawlish took pity on him.

'And there's another thing,' he went on. 'I don't know where you got the idea that I'm a free agent, but it's erroneous. I might conceivably play hide-and-seek with the police, but only if I thought it was the only way of getting satisfactory results. I know them well, I'm unofficially attached to them, and I can make no guarantees at all.'

Bingham dropped into his chair, like a deflated balloon.

'I – I can hardly believe it,' he muttered.

'Well, it's true,' said Dawlish gently. 'And there's another thing – I work for my living. Or if you prefer it, I'm in the army. That doesn't give me a lot of spare time. Don't you think you've come to the wrong address?'

'Wrong – wrong address?' muttered Bingham, looking completely crushed. 'I – I had quite the wrong conception, quite the wrong one, that is obvious. But – but you *must* help. No one else will be able to do as much as you, I am convinced of that.'

'You might be wrong there, too,' Dawlish pointed out.

'But I am not, there is no question of appealing to anyone else, it – it is a matter in which you are already involved.' Bingham was labouring under considerable emotion; he looked at his cheque book in bewilderment. 'Major Dawlish, a friend, a very dear friend of mine, is in great need of help. *Great* need. I do not know the full circumstances, but I do understand that for private reasons she is most reluctant to consult the police. She – she has already consulted you, but at that time did not know how dangerous were the paths which she had chosen to tread. You doubtless know whom I mean?'

'Amelia Shortt, yes,' said Dawlish.

'Then you must know how deserving she is of help,' cried Bingham. 'That sweet child, so confused, so harassed, so worried – Dawlish, you had already promised to help her. You will not fail her now, I am sure.'

Dawlish repressed a temptation to make a terse remark, and said briskly:

'Why come to me waving a cheque book, Bingham? If you'd told me what you wanted in the first place, and explained the telephone call you made to me, I would have been more impressed.'

'Please!' explained Bingham, holding up a supplicatory hand. 'I am fully aware of the clumsiness of my approach, but as I have told you the matter is now much more serious than it was earlier today. I wanted to ensure that I could get assistance for Amelia of such a kind that she would not be disappointed. I thought that if I paid you a large enough fee you would take – er – take my instructions, and that a man of your reputation would not fail to produce the required results. Now it is obvious that I shall have to completely revise my opinions and my approach to you.'

'Good,' said Dawlish. 'Where is Amelia?'

Bingham drew a deep breath.

'That is one of the most disturbing factors, Major Dawlish. I do not know.' He paused. 'A short while before I telephoned you I spoke to Amelia also by telephone. She gave me to understand that something had gone amiss, and that she would not be able to return to London tonight. She asked me to dissuade you from going to the Jermyn Street house, but not to do anything which would rob you of your interest in her affairs. I did that, to the best of my ability.'

Dawlish nodded, only half-convinced.

'I manufactured the story of a minor accident to Amelia, and the statement that her father had gone to see her,' said Bingham in a low voice, 'because I thought that was the most satisfactory way of dealing with the matter. I had arranged to meet her a little later in the evening, and I went to meet her a little later in the evening, and I went to the appointed *rendezvous*. She did not appear. I knew how important a matter the meeting was to have been for her, and I was most anxious. Then I had a telephone message. She told me that her father had – er – ' Bingham gulped again – 'been kidnapped, Major Dawlish. She had just time to tell me that, and then I heard her exclaim as if in alarm. A man's voice followed, and then the receiver went dead.' Bingham brushed a hand across his forehead. 'I am sure you can imagine my horror, Major Dawlish. I did not know what to do. I – I should tell you that Amelia charged me, in that last tragic telephone call, to say nothing of this to the police. I knew of your interest and your fame – and I thought that I could best approach you as I did. But although I made so distressing a mistake, I hope, I trust, I can still rely on your help.'

Dawlish said: 'Did you know that Amelia was going to approach me earlier?'

'Oh, yes. In fact I – er – I suggested it.'

'Why?' asked Dawlish.

'Because I was so convinced that you were the one man who could help her,' said Bingham desperately. 'A friend – I should perhaps say an acquaintance – of mine was once in a most difficult situation, and you helped him. He had a most firmly established faith in you. Major Dawlish, I implore you not to keep me on tenterhooks any longer. You *will* help? You *must* help! For I am frightened of the consequences of this strange mystery. I – I should tell you that a man has been murdered – *murdered* – under my very eyes!'

Chapter 7

Dawlish Says 'Yes'

A man had been murdered, thought Dawlish, in the sight of Bingham. Judging from the pallor of the man's face he did not consider that an exaggeration.

'Who was murdered, Bingham? And where?'

'An – an old servant of Dr Shortt's. At – at Jermyn Street. Dawlish, will you — '

Dawlish said abruptly: 'Yes, I'll help where I can, but whether it will be the way you want it is a different matter. The police know about that murder, they're busy on it now. Someone telephoned them from Jermyn Street.' His eyes were fixed on Bingham's. 'Was it you?'

'Y-yes,' admitted Bingham with a gulp. 'I knew that I could not allow it to happen without advising the police, but I had little opportunity for talking to them, and – and – ' He broke off, while Dawlish eyed him with a hint of amusement.

'Now we're getting at the truth, Bingham.'

'What – what do you mean?'

'That you came along here with an offer of limitless money for your own sake, not Amelia's.'

Bingham goggled at him.

'I – I assure you, Major Dawlish – '

'Look here,' said Dawlish with sudden irritation, 'you were at the house and you saw Kibb killed. You telephoned the police but gave them only the vaguest of clues to the scene of the murder. There's just one reason for that – you're afraid that you will be suspected of having killed Kibb. Don't lie about it. If you didn't kill him you've nothing to fear.'

'I – I wish I could be sure of that.'

'It's why you came here, isn't it?' demanded Dawlish.

'Yes. Yes, I suppose subconsciously that was the main reason, but I do assure you that all I have told you about

47

Amelia was true, and that I should not have been at the house but for my anxiety to be of assistance to her. Major Dawlish, I have had a most distressing, a most frightening experience. I will tell you everything. I – I went to the house, entering with a key which Amelia lent me, to get some papers from her room. I had arranged to do that much earlier in the evening. When I arrived, when I reached her room, I was aware of the presence of others.'

Bingham broke off, and gulped again. Dawlish made no interruption, although he thought fleetingly of the impatience which Beresford would now be sharing with Hubbard.

'I did not know them – I could not even see them,' said Bingham in a low voice. 'They went upstairs, towards Dr Shortt's laboratory. Kibb came out of his room – I was on a landing, and could see exactly what happened. The courageous fellow immediately closed with the men – there were three of them. I *saw* one of them use a knife.' Bingham shuddered, and Dawlish wondered fleetingly whether a man could act as well as this, or whether he was relating the literal truth. On the whole he plumped for the latter.

'And this happened on the landing?' asked Dawlish.

'That is so.' Bingham nodded. 'In front of my very eyes, Major Dawlish. And – and in my alarm I retired into another room. You may think that cowardly, but – well, Kibb was undoubtedly dead, and there were three men there.'

'Yes,' said Dawlish. 'It's understandable.'

'I make no excuse for my behaviour,' said Bingham with a simplicity which Dawlish found disarming. 'I wish that I had the physical courage which some men possess, but I feel convinced that I would have done no good had I declared myself.'

'Probably not,' agreed Dawlish.

'You see, I realised that Dr Shortt had been alarmed, and I actually heard him close, and lock, the door of his laboratory,' said Bingham. 'He has a telephone there. I felt sure that he would be able to send for help. In the room where I took refuge, however, I could hear little, and for most of the time I was by the window. I thought that I might be able to get out that way, but it was too high for me, and I gave up the attempt.' Bingham paused dramatically. 'By then, the top floor was empty of people. The door of the laboratory was open, and Dr Shortt was not there. I went to the

48

laboratory and telephoned the police. I realised that I was in a most invidious position, and – and I hurried away. After much consideration I decided to come and tell you the whole story.'

'And you have?' asked Dawlish gently.

'I have indeed,' Bingham assured him.

'I think not,' said Dawlish gently.

Bingham stared at him, his eyes widening.

'I – I beg your pardon?'

'I said that you had not told me the whole story,' Dawlish told him. 'You see, Bingham, I've seen affairs like this before and there are certain well-worn modes of behaviour. One of them is, that under the circumstances you have described to me, a man of average intelligence would not run away from the house because of fear of suspicion. There was no reason at all why you shouldn't call the police, and wait for them to substantiate your story.'

Bingham drew a deep breath.

'What – what do you mean?'

'Now, come,' said Dawlish with a touch of impatience. 'Why were you so anxious not to be seen on the premises? Was it because of your friendship with Amelia?'

Bingham stared at him for several seconds without speaking, and then said very deliberately:

'No, Dawlish, it was not. You see, I – I am a humble contemporary, I might almost say a disciple, of Dr Shortt's. Unfortunately, we did not always see eye to eye. There was a time when I was an assistant in his laboratory, but we – er – quarrelled violently. Although friendly with Amelia, I was forbidden the house. I – I was afraid of what the police might make of that unsatisfactory and unfortunate relationship. I was guided then by selfish motives only, I fear.'

Dawlish was tempted to ask the reasons for the quarrel between Bingham and Dr Shortt, but he decided that he had contrived to get as much as he could reasonably expect out of the plump man that evening. And there were other, more urgent considerations. There was little doubt, if Bingham's story were true and he did not see any reason for disbelieving it in general outline, that Shortt had been kidnapped: and the odds were that the same misfortune had befallen Amelia.

Those things were urgent.

He did not propose to tell Bingham how deeply he was involved with the police. If he kept the story back from

Trivett it would not be for Bingham's sake, but because he thought that it might be wise, and contribute eventually to the smoothing out of the complications. He felt neither friendliness nor animosity towards Bingham.

'You – you will help?' Bingham asked again.

'I've said so,' Dawlish reminded him. 'You've no idea where Amelia telephoned you from?'

'No, none at all.'

'Have you any idea of the reason for Dr Shortt's recent sleeplessness and anxiety?' went on Dawlish, allowing it to be assumed for the time being that he believed that part of the story which Amelia had told him.

'Only that Amelia considered he was being blackmailed,' declared Bingham.

'And the identity of the blackmailers?'

'A complete mystery,' Bingham assured him.

Dawlish doubted it, without putting his doubts into words. He believed that both Amelia and Bingham knew more of what was going on – or had been going on – than they admitted, but it was no time to develop that angle, except in so far as it might help him to find who had visited the Jermyn Street house. He did not think that he would get any information, direct or indirect, by further questioning, and so he said:

'I see. All right, Bingham. I'll have your address and telephone number, and – '

'What are you going to do?' demanded Bingham eagerly.

'I don't know,' admitted Dawlish.

'Have you *any* ideas which might be fruitful?'

'None at all,' Dawlish assured him.

Bingham took a card from his wallet and extended it towards the big man.

He read:

> Dr C. J. Bingham,
> 8a Appleton Mansions,
> South Kensington, S.W.7.

There were many doubts in Dawlish's mind, not the least concerning Bingham's account of his own part in the affair, but he spoke the truth when he said that he had no constructive ideas at all. For that matter he did not see that anyone could have derived ideas from his present information. But he had succeeded in making Bingham think that he was fully satisfied with the story, and therefore set the man's mind at rest. That was a start which could lead to many things.

He said slowly: 'Excuse me just a moment, will you?'

Leaving Bingham in the dining-room, he stepped into the lounge and pulled the door to without closing it. Beresford was sprawling back in an easy chair, his eyes half-closed. Hubbard, more on edge, was standing by the mantelshelf.

Hubbard said: 'Well, what – '

'Hush,' murmured Dawlish. He took a pencil from his pocket and scrawled on the back of Bingham's card: *Go to his flat, watch him arrive.* That done he dropped the card on Beresford's lap, and went back to the dining-room.

Hubbard was astonished at the speed with which Beresford hoisted himself from his chair. He was actually out of the lounge before Dawlish reached the dining-room door.

'I've been looking through my notes of what Amelia told me,' said Dawlish mendaciously, a hand at his pocket as if he were in the act of replacing them. 'It fits in fairly well with your story, Bingham. Meanwhile there's just one other thing. Do you know Manchester at all?'

Bingham stared at him.

'Manchester? Slightly, yes.'

'Does Mere Street, Number 81, mean anything to you?' asked Dawlish.

He did not expect to get the slightest reaction, and was in fact only talking to give Ted ample time to get to Appleton Mansions before the plump doctor. But hardly was the name 'Mere Street' out of his mouth when he realised that it did mean something.

'*Mere* Street!' gasped Bingham. 'Why – ' He stopped, at a loss for words.

'Well, what about it?' asked Dawlish as mildly as he could.

'How on earth do you know about *Mere* Street?' demanded Bingham. 'I thought it was an absolute secret. I had no idea, I – ' Bingham leapt from his chair and gripped Dawlish's forearm. 'If you have discovered the Mere Street house you are *all* that your reputation says. I cannot understand it. I can hardly believe you have uttered that word!'

Dawlish accepted the laudation without batting an eye.

'Well, what is it?' he demanded.

'It – er – it – ' Bingham licked his lips again. 'It is a pri-

51

vate nursing home, Dawlish. Dr Shortt has several experimental cases there, some unfortunate war victims whom he is endeavouring to bring back to full life, mental and physical. But he has refused anyone – *any*one access to the place. I think one of his great fears was that I should talk of it when I left him, although I hope that my discretion and loyalty to such a man is strong enough to withstand any such temptation. But *Mere* Street. Dawlish, how did you discover it?'

'It was just one of those things,' said Dawlish, but although he smiled and ushered Bingham towards the door, he felt quite certain that the youthful doctor had received a shock, and was more than disturbed at the very idea that Dawlish knew of the Mere Street nursing home.

Chapter 8

81 Mere Street

Dawlish felt a little satisfaction when Bingham had gone, although it was small enough.

He had in any case intended to make tentative inquiries about the house in Mere Street to which he and Felicity had been directed. As it was, Bingham had so sharpened the appeal of the place that he decided to take the first train next morning to Manchester.

He told Hubbard of this, and further troubled that disappointed sailor, who said with some justification:

'But why on earth go to Manchester? That's just where the people who sent those telegrams wanted you to go.'

'Is it?' asked Dawlish thoughtfully.

'Of course it is! That's what you said yourself.'

Dawlish smiled at him, and considered.

The pseudo-telegrams had been sent with a purpose. He had considered himself very smart when he had spotted a motive behind them. Now he wondered whether it had been the correct one.

Had the sender seriously expected both Felicity and himself to go to 81, Mere Street – or had his aim been to hammer the address into Dawlish's mind? And – an even less pleasing thought – had the sender felt quite sure that sooner or later Dawlish would go to Manchester?

That was at least possible.

Hubbard, who might be ingenuous and a little wearisome was no fool. He jumped to the obvious conclusion, and nine times out of ten it was the right one. Allowing that, if Dawlish went to Manchester it would be exactly what the sender of the telegrams wanted.

He was puzzled, also, by the obvious concern with which Bingham viewed his discovery of the place. It had jolted the man.

'It looks just a mess, to me,' declared Hubbard.

Dawlish agreed with him.

'But why on earth you should go to Manchester when it's just what they want you to do, I can't imagine,' went on Hubbard aggrievedly. 'Didn't Bingham tell you anything that might help?'

'Not substantially,' admitted Dawlish.

It was at this point that Beresford telephoned from a kiosk in Exhibition Road to tell him that Bingham had reached his flat. Ted had not been idle, but had discovered that Appleton Mansions was one of the few places which still boasted a night porter, an old and decrepit man who had not been averse to talking. Beresford had exchanged notes with him, and been told that Bingham was a very 'nice' gentleman, generous and polite, unlike many of the other tenants, and that he had a practice at the Mansions.

'A medical practice?' Dawlish was surprised.

'There's a brass plate, anyhow,' said Beresford. 'And apparently it's a big practice, bearing in mind that there aren't so many doctors left in London now. He's been here for eighteen months, and believe me, he's no pauper. The flats are the luxurious kind.'

'I'd gathered that,' admitted Dawlish, thinking of the five thousand pounds. 'What type of clients?'

'Obviously the well-to-do. He's got another, poorer, surgery near South Kensington Station, which he shares with three others, all much older men according to the porter.'

'One wonders why Bingham hasn't been called up,' mused Dawlish. 'Trivett could probably give the reason, but I'm not sure that this is a matter for Bill yet. We'll see. I wish –' He broke off, realising just in time that he was about to say that he wished Tim Jeremy were there. Tim was another old and tried friend, but Hubbard might take such a remark amiss.

'What shall I do?' asked Beresford.

'You might as well come back here,' said Dawlish. 'Give him half-an-hour. If he hasn't had a visitor, or gone out, in that time, he's probably gone to bed.'

He replaced the receiver, and caught Hubbard in the midst of a gargantuan yawn. He suggested that they, too, repaired to bed. Reluctantly, and still making his disillusionment obvious, Hubbard agreed, and Dawlish gave him the small single room. In spite of his objections, Hubbard was

54

asleep before Beresford had returned.

'Nothing doing?' asked Dawlish.

'Not a thing. Did you get anything out of him?'

'I don't know,' admitted Dawlish.

While they were undressing he gave Beresford a résumé of Bingham's statement. Snug in one of the twin beds, Beresford said sleepily:

'So you're going to Manchester?'

'Yes.'

'Am I coming?'

'I think you'd better keep Hubbard occupied down here with inquiries about Bingham,' said Dawlish. 'He'll probably give himself away, and I don't think that will matter.'

It was, Dawlish decided when the light was out and he lay looking up towards the window through which a faint peppering of stars were visible, a most unsatisfactory position. Although Bingham had appeared to be frank enough, there remained the possibility that like Amelia he was being guileful. It remained a fact, moreover, that Amelia had conspired with Bingham to interest Dawlish, although Bingham had not said much about that. He had passed the position skilfully, and Dawlish wondered why.

He was awakened by Hubbard, just after eight o'clock.

At the chink of cups Beresford awoke quickly, blinking about him.

'What's that I see? Tea? Great Lord deliver us, Hubbard's human!'

'As a matter of fact,' admitted Hubbard somewhat self-consciously, 'I've an uncomfortable feeling that I made a fool of myself last night, Dawlish. I – er – I rather romanticised the business, if you know what I mean. Sorry and all that. I hope I haven't damned myself for good and all.'

'Good heavens, old boy,' said Beresford comfortably. 'Pat's methods need more than a day and a night to come to terms with, without getting violent indigestion. You'll get used to them. You might even admire them. I'll have that lump of sugar if no one wants it. Any brainwaves, Pat?'

'None,' said Dawlish regretfully. 'But I think we'll do the obvious thing and see what happens.'

A train left for Manchester at half-past nine. Before leaving for the station, Dawlish telephoned first Clay House, to be told that there had been no message for him, and then to Scotland Yard.

Trivett reported that the Manchester address had proved to be occupied by a reputable Mancunian, who had lived there for the past thirty years.

'Hm,' said Dawlish. 'Well, that was the most likely thing to find, wasn't it? Provided, of course, that it was a real address in the first place. Did you speak to Felicity's C.O.?'

'Yes. It's all right – Felicity will be on duty until six o'clock this evening. Then she's going to get in touch with you.'

'Good man,' said Dawlish.

'Has anything happened your end?' demanded Trivett.

'Yes,' said Dawlish emphatically. 'We've had a good night's sleep, and that counts for a lot. Cheerio, Bill.'

The information about 81, Mere Street was not wholly surprising to Dawlish: Bingham had made it clear that Dr Shortt had maintained such secrecy about the place that, to all formal inquiries, an obvious and satisfying answer would be available. The more he pondered over Mere Street, the more Dawlish liked the idea of going there.

The journey to Manchester was surprisingly good, and on arrival he found a better supply of taxis than at most London termini. By two-fifteen Dawlish had finished a good lunch at a restaurant of renown, and was supplied with a street directory by a considerate waitress. The fact that he was in uniform probably accounted for the ease with which he acquired all these things, for he had deliberately chosen to wear it for that very reason.

Mere Street, he discovered, was a small residential thoroughfare. He took a taxi to a nearby avenue, paid off the driver, and walked the rest of the way.

There was very little that was modern about Mere Street. Its houses were tall and grey while plane trees, refreshed by a recent shower of rain, pleasantly shaded the road.

Dawlish turned and walked away from Number 81, deciding to weigh up the situation before taking action. When he reached the corner he saw a little man hurrying along the street, hatless, dressed in black, his face flushed by exertion. Dawlish contemplated him casually, wondering what urgent mission had brought the man out.

He did not wonder for long, for the little man stopped dead in front of him.

'Excuse me, sir, but – aren't you Major Dawlish?'

Chapter 9

Dawlish Is Astonished

'I – I hope I haven't made a mistake,' the man went on nervously. 'You *are* Major Dawlish, aren't you?'

'Yes,' said Dawlish slowly.

'Ah, then I am lucky indeed. I have been waiting for you all the morning – what delayed you?'

Dawlish temporised quickly: 'I missed a train.'

'What a pity,' said the little man, putting a hand on his arm. 'Come with me, please, sir. We shall all be very glad to see you, believe me. It is a great relief to know that you are here, a great relief.'

They reached the entrance to Number 81.

The door stood open; beyond it was a high-ceilinged, narrow passage. Dawlish entered slowly, wondering whether he was a fool to take what the little fellow said for granted. If this man was right, he, and some other, had been expecting him, and were on tenterhooks because he had arrived so late.

Until he knew why, he would have to feel his way along.

But he was wary, especially when the door closed, leaving only a faint glow from a landing window. The little man, still with a hand on Dawlish's arm, started for the stairs.

He had said little since his greeting, but now began to chatter volubly.

'We were immensely relieved when we knew that you were coming. We really did not know what to do, nor which way to turn. Such a tragedy – or perhaps I should say a potential tragedy. We must find the doctor, Major Dawlish.'

'Ah,' said Dawlish. So they knew Shortt was missing.

'And it was kind of you to wire so promptly,' said the little man. 'It relieved us of a great deal of anxiety. You see, Miss Amelia has told us about you, she knows how capable you are.' In the gloom of the landing the man looked up at Dawlish and smiled: it was the face of a child more than a man, trustful, open.

'So I telegraphed that I was coming,' thought Dawlish in astonishment. 'We're getting on.'

'It's such an utter mystery,' continued the little man, 'and we are all at a loss to understand it. Who should wish to harm Dr Shortt, or to delay his valuable work? It is incomprehensible.'

'Yes, indeed,' said Dawlish.

'But I must not talk so freely.' The man paused by a door leading to the right of the passage. 'I shall leave that to Mr Posslethwaite – did Miss Amelia mention him?'

'No,' said Dawlish.

'She is very discreet, I know,' admitted the other. 'Perhaps she omitted to mention my name, also?' He paused with a hand on the door knob. 'Ah, I can tell that she did from your expression. I am Jones.'

He flung open the door. In that there was a gesture of some deliberation, almost triumph.

'Major Dawlish has arrived.'

Dawlish stepped into a long, sun-filled room as another voice, heavy with Lancashire dialect, greeted him.

'Ah'm very glad to see you, Major.'

Sitting by the window which overlooked the street was a powerfully-built man who made no attempt to rise. As his eyes became accustomed to the sunlight, Dawlish saw that Posslethwaite was sitting in an invalid chair. He extended his right hand, and Dawlish took it. The grip was powerful: whatever ailment incapacitated Posslethwaite, it did not affect his hand or arm. He gave a deep, rumbling laugh.

'Right up your street, a case like this, Ah will say. And we're fortunate to have such a man wi' us, Major. Sit down now.' He stretched towards a box of cigarettes and pushed them nearer to Dawlish. 'Have you had your lunch?'

'Thanks, yes,' said Dawlish weakly.

'That's good,' declared Posslethwaite, 'but Ah might have known you wouldn't waste time. You're like one of us, Major, you like to get on wi' it.'

Dawlish shifted his chair, which had been placed so that the sun shone in his eyes. He moved into shadow, and was able to see Posslethwaite more clearly. The other had a heavy face, a reddish complexion, and an air of almost leisurely composure. Dawlish liked him on sight, just as he had liked Jones, although with the little man there was a hint of amusement in his attitude.

Posslethwaite was in a different category. He was a man of intelligence and perhaps of intellect. Dawlish wondered again what afflicted him.

'Well, now you've sized me up, what do you make of me?' demanded the invalid humorously.

For the first time Dawlish smiled: he felt a touch of kinship with this man.

'You'll do,' he said briefly. 'Whether *I* will, is a different matter.' He glanced at Jones, and at last took a cigarette from the box. 'I didn't send a wire,' he said. 'I didn't know I would be expected. Nor did I hear of Mere Street from Amelia Shortt.'

Posslethwaite stiffened in his chair, his powerful left hand gripped the wheel more tightly. But it was Jones who exclaimed in a high-pitched voice:

'But I have your wire *here*! I have it in my pocket!'

'It didn't come from me,' said Dawlish calmly, 'but I am prepared to believe that you thought it did.'

Posslethwaite said slowly: 'Ah think Ah know when a man's telling the truth, Major.'

'But – ' began Jones, agitatedly.

'Hold your peace, man,' said Posslethwaite sharply, 'there's no time for blethering. Ah'll believe what you say Major, but Ah'll ask you to be good enough to tell me why you did come here. Ah didn't know so many people were aware of the address.'

Dawlish wondered whether to introduce the name of Bingham, but decided against it. The time might come when he would have to tell these people everything he knew, but for the time being essentials were enough. He was disconcertingly aware of the shrewdness of the invalid's gaze: Posslethwaite would not be easily deceived.

'How did you learn of it?' Posslethwaite's voice hardened. 'You'll be telling me next that Amelia didn't approach you.'

'Oh, Amelia approached me all right,' said Dawlish, 'and then someone tried, or I thought they tried, to head me off. Do you know how Shortt was kidnapped?'

'No,' said Posslethwaite, and waited in silent invitation.

Briefly, Dawlish told him what had happened at Jermyn Street, omitting Bingham's confessions, concentrating only on what he had done as a consequence of Amelia's appeal. Because he gathered that Amelia was in favour at Mere Street he did not criticise her, even by implication. Judging

59

Posslethwaite to be a sound judge of character he was a little puzzled that she had not been dismissed by him as casually as by Dr Grayling. There was, he thought sadly, every chance that Posslethwaite had been deceived by a pretty face.

He wasted no words in his narrative, which was interrupted only by agitated clucks from Jones, and finished casually enough.

'Since someone obviously wanted me to come to Mere Street, here I am. I expected' – he paused, weighing his words carefully – 'I expected a hostile reception. I thought that it was an exceptionally clever bait, covered by its very obviousness.'

Posslethwaite allowed himself a grim smile.

'Aye, Ah've that kind of mind too, Major. But if you thought that was behind it, why come up t'place?' His dialect grew broader, he was obviously deep in the web of circumstances which Dawlish had outlined.

'Wilful obstinacy,' said Dawlish, smiling. 'Presumably I was the fish, Mere Street the bait. Now and again a fish might get curious enough to want to see what's at the end of the line that holds the hook that holds the bait. Sometimes the fish can get the bait out of its mouth before there's any danger. I like to think that I can. Big-headedness, you see.'

'Aye, Ah know it,' said Posslethwaite, still with the grim unamused smile. 'It's the kind of thing Ah like to hear, Major. You're not easily scared Ah'll declare. But we've summat to think about now. Why did they want you to come here? Aye,' he added heavily, 'and what do they propose to do now that you are here? That's the question, and Ah don't know that Ah like it.'

Dawlish said softly: 'No. Presumably they think I'm in their way. Could you be, too?'

'Ah think so,' admitted Posslethwaite softly. 'Ah think Ah'm beginning to see the light, Major, but the day'll come when the deal wi' those bellyachin' scoundrels will be different to what they expect.' He spoke gently, but his general demeanour made Dawlish more conscious of danger than he had been since the start of the affair. 'And Ah think we'll go out,' added Posslethwaite. 'Jones, fetch my hat and coat, will you?'

'But – ' began Jones.

'Go on with you,' roared Posslethwaite, his voice making

the air quiver. 'Stop hopping from one foot to another like a demented old woman.'

Jones skipped agilely across the room, and as the door closed behind him Posslethwaite smiled with a gleam of genuine humour. It faded quickly.

'Dawlish, Ah've something of importance t' say t'you. Happen we'll get through this lot all right, and if we do then Ah'll have time t'tell you more of what all this is about, but if anything happens to me you'll find all the notes Ah've made about it in a box at the Riall Safe Deposit.' He took a key from his waistcoat pocket, handed it to Dawlish, and added quickly: 'Ah've arranged with the manager of my bank that if you see him and show him the key he'll take you to the Riall. Don't waste time wi' questions now, we're in a hurry. Now –'

'What's likely to happen to you?' Dawlish demanded.

Again Posslethwaite showed that grim, half-humorous smile.

'Ask Jones or anyone who knows me well, Dawlish. Ah'm halfway t'me grave a'reet, and Ah'll pop off one of these days before you can say "snap". A sudden shock is likely to do it, or exertion, and happen Ah'll have to exert myself before the day's out.'

Before Dawlish could speak Jones came back.

'Be careful now, Mr Posslethwaite, don't overdo it.'

'Give me the coat,' growled Posslethwaite. 'And –'

He was looking towards the little man, but Dawlish was watching him, wondering how much of this was an act put on for his benefit; it was not safe to take anything for granted, not even the gruff downrightness of the man in the invalid chair.

He saw Posslethwaite's smile grow tense, and changed the direction of his gaze swiftly. He saw past Jones, who stood with mouth agape, staring at Posslethwaite but obviously affected by the man's expression. He saw the door opening, and was on his feet in a moment.

Two men entered, one holding a gun, the other with a handkerchief tied over the lower half of his face.

Chapter 10

'No Joke,' Says Dawlish

The thing which angered Dawlish was the unexpectedness of it. All that had happened at Jermyn Street should have prepared him for such measures, for a ruthlessness which would leave him little room for mistakes and careless risks.

Then he wondered whether he could have done much about it in any case, and concentrated on appraising the two men.

He saw at once that the man with the gun was there as a guard; the man who mattered was he with the spotted blue and red handkerchief over his nose, mouth and chin.

He spoke into a tense silence.

'Good afternoon, gentlemen.'

The man with the gun glanced at him, his little eyes expressionless. The other ignored him.

'Posslethwaite, you know what I want. Where is it?'

'Happen Ah don't know,' said Posslethwaite with commendable calmness.

'You know, and you'll talk.'

'Ah don't think so,' said Posslethwaite. 'Let me tell you, ma lad, Ah'm not trading with you now or at any time in the future. Ah don't give a snap of the fingers for you.'

'That might be true,' the other conceded, while Dawlish watched and waited in the background, 'but you do for others. Amelia Shortt, for instance.'

'Ah,' said Posslethwaite. The ejaculation seemed forced from his lips. Dawlish looked at him and saw the swelling veins on his forehead, others standing out on the backs of his hands where he gripped his chair. 'Ah'll teach you – ' he began.

'Please, please!' gasped Jones. 'Don't excite yourself, sir, don't excite yourself, you know what might happen! You won't do any good by talking that way. Please!'

'Very good advice,' said the man with the mask. 'Relax,

Posslethwaite. You'll give me what I want, or the woman – '

Dawlish said gently: 'Dear me, this is all rather elementary, isn't it?'

He succeeded in distracting the man's attention, saw Posslethwaite look towards him with some relaxing of tension. He went on:

'After all, kidnapping, hostages, threats – it's all very old stuff. Didn't anyone ever tell you that, out of a paper-backed novel, it never comes off?' He beamed.

The other raised his head to look at him, and Dawlish caught a glimpse of glittering eyes, and felt another flash of satisfaction, for he was holding the man's attention. Dawlish's main object was to gain time. He was in a fog of uncertainty, knowing only that there was menace and more than menace in the presence of the two men.

'Let us put an end to such highly-coloured nonsense,' he added lightly. 'As a matter of fact, the matter is in my hands. It would be better if you dealt with me direct in future, and not with my principals!'

Even Posslethwaite gasped.

The glittering eyes, still visible, seemed to narrow. The man with the gun took a step forward, and Dawlish very much disliked the casualness with which he raised the weapon.

He could not be sure that the gunman would hold his fire long enough for him to say what he wanted; and yet he did not hurry, for he was anxious to create the impression that he was completely confident of himself, and dealing with accomplished facts.

'It's a good thing for them that they did come to me. The police – '

Until the word 'police' the man had been raising his gun slowly, and it was almost possible to see him deliberating on the most vulnerable part of Dawlish's body. On the word, he moved abruptly for the first time, taking a quick step forward. Posslethwaite drew in a sharp breath.

Quickly though Dawlish looked away, he was unable to evade the grip of the masked man's fingers on his forearm, nor the prodding of the other's gun in his right side. He was crowded against the wall, and although he relaxed his muscles without straining or trying to resist, the pain was considerable.

'Don't lie to me,' the man said evenly. 'You haven't seen

the police, Posslethwaite wouldn't let you.'

'I like my own methods,' said Dawlish, looking undaunted into the masked face. Inwardly he rejoiced, despite the threat of the gun in his ribs. 'Of course I've seen the police. I was with Trivett at the Yard for an hour last night. I told him where I was coming today, and unless he –'

He broke off abruptly and set his lips.

There was a moment of utter silence, while the gun ground painfully into his ribs and the pressure of the bony fingers increased. The voice of the masked man came thinly.

'Unless what? Go on.'

'Be damned to you!' snapped Dawlish. 'I've said too much as it is.'

'Unless *what?*' repeated the masked man, and increased his pressure.

Dawlish felt a beading of sweat at his forehead and the nape of his neck. But that did not matter; the thing of importance was that he had compelled their interest, had them so curious that they would make him answer and when he answered would believe that he spoke the truth because he talked so obviously against his will.

'It's no use –' he began.

'You . . . ' said the man with the gun viciously.

He doubled his knee and brought it up into the pit of Dawlish's stomach, a movement so sudden and vicious that Dawlish gasped aloud with the agony which seared through his body. He sagged downwards, but was kept up by the bony hand; he saw the glittering anger of the masked man's eyes, felt a buffet on the side of the head which made his ears ring.

'What were you going to say?'

'I'm damned if I'll –' began Dawlish.

Another buffet brought tears to his eyes, the pain at his wrist grew worse: and then the gunman, forsaking his weapon, gripped Dawlish's right hand, took the little finger, and began to force it back. The pain was lost in the agony of the rest, but it was enough to justify Dawlish in shouting:

'Stop it, stop it!'

There was a slight easing of the pressure. He drew in a deep breath, felt a bead of sweat trickle down his forehead into his eye. He saw the others through a mist, and yet was conscious of deep satisfaction, for they were completely deceived.

'Now talk,' said the man with the mask. 'What did you arrange with the police?'

'I – I told them where I was coming, and – '

'We know that. Don't waste our time. What were they going to do?'

Dawlish gasped: 'Follow me, of course, they – they always do. I saw Munk at the station, he – '

'Who's Munk?'

'Trivett's sergeant,' said Dawlish, as if he had cracked completely. 'Let me go, I can't stand it any longer, let me go!'

'Who's Trivett?' demanded the man with the mask, without relaxing his pressure.

'Su-Superintendent Trivett at Scotland Yard,' gasped Dawlish.

The man released him then, flinging him back so that he hit the wall, and then sagged forward against Posslethwaite's chair.

In spite of the mist in his mind and the pain which went through his whole body, Dawlish felt curiously light-hearted. There was a new urgency about the manner of the inquisitors, they were trying to rush results, in fear that the police were, or would be, watching the house.

The masked man seized Posslethwaite's hand and began to bend the fingers backwards.

Then Dawlish, quite simply, put a hand on the wheel of the invalid chair, and eased the brake off. It clicked back, and the heavy chair moved forward. As the surprised gun-man leapt out of the way, Dawlish straightened up and with a satisfaction which added strength to his arm, struck him a resounding blow on the side of the head.

It would have been powerful enough to have sent the man to the floor in any case. As it was he struck against Posslethwaite's tormentor, and they both hit the floor simultaneously. Dawlish bent down and very simply took the gun from the floor.

He felt very much better as he knelt on one knee by the side of the masked man, and pulled the spotted handkerchief down. He paid little attention to the livid face beyond it, the glittering eyes set deep and close, but began to go through the man's pockets. Dawlish took a wallet, several letters, a fountain pen, loose silver, keys, and put them by his side on the floor. Only when he was finished did he straighten up.

Jones had done an equally sound job on the gunman, and now looked at Dawlish with glowing eyes.

'He – he hasn't got anything else, sir, he – '

Jones turned towards Posslethwaite, obviously to share his elation, but his expression altered. He leapt to his feet with an exclamation of alarm.

And he had good cause.

Posslethwaite's head was slumped forward on his chest. His whole body sagged. His hands flopped pallidly over the sides of the chair, and there was nothing to indicate movement or life in him.

With a despairing cry Jones dashed out of the room. Quietly Dawlish picked up the oddments from the floor, and, selecting the tall man's wallet, began to look through it. He saw several new visiting cards. There was no address, but the name was: *Fanessa*.

Before Dawlish had time to look at the several letters which came from the wallet, Jones rushed back. He carried a hypodermic syringe in his right hand. Reaching Posslethwaite he bent over him solicitously.

'Any chance?' asked Dawlish, gently.

'It – it might just be in time,' said Jones with tears in his eyes. 'If it isn't – if it isn't – '

He turned towards the men on the floor. Although Dawlish saw the way his face had lost its colour, and the glitter in his eyes, he was taken completely by surprise. For Jones rushed at the two men and kicked at them savagely, wildly, caring nothing where his shoes struck them. The thuds of the blows, mingling with the sudden cries of the attacked men, merged in a medley of discord which filled the room.

Dawlish jumped forward, and gripped the back of Jones's neck. The man continued to kick, completely ignoring him, but as Dawlish tightened his grip his kicks grew weaker until at last Dawlish dragged him away.

It had not been a pleasant interlude.

Dawlish released him, and said quietly: 'That kind of thing won't help, you know.'

Jones drew in a deep, searing breath, but said nothing. There was a film of tears in his eyes, and he was shaking from head to foot. Dawlish urged him into a chair, where he sat looking at Posslethwaite with the expression of a faithful dog looking at a beloved master. It was as if Jones had bared his very soul and revealed that all he cared for was Posslethwaite, the big, helpless man tied to that wheelchair.

The man with the handkerchief now drooped about his neck spoke urgently.

'Dawlish, I've got to go.'

'That's a thought,' said Dawlish. 'It hasn't occurred to me.'

'I tell you I've got to go! I'll make it worth your while, I'll pay you – ' He paused, and then went on with a gasp: 'I'll pay you five hundred pounds to let me go!'

'First threats and coercion, and now bribery and corruption,' murmured Dawlish. 'Before you start anything like this you should really take lessons, you know. I'm not for sale.'

'If – if anything prevents me getting back, the girl will – will suffer.'

'You suggested that before,' said Dawlish. 'And on that I might come to terms. Only might, mind you,' he added. 'The terms being you in exchange for Amelia, Amelia to come first. Is that clear enough?'

The man licked his lips.

'I – I can't guarantee – '

'That's too bad,' interrupted Dawlish, 'because your only chance of not spending the night in a police cell is the return of Amelia, uninjured. The only chance, Fanessa.'

'I can't be sure they – they'll release her,' the man muttered.

'That's too bad.'

'I – I'll try.'

'Thoughtful of you,' said Dawlish. 'How do you propose to do that?'

'By telephone.'

Dawlish glanced about the study, and saw the telephone on a small shelf built against the wall. He nodded towards it. The man dragged himself, groaning, to his feet, and lifted the receiver. He spoke softly obviously trying to give the number without Dawlish hearing him.

He succeeded in this, but he had to repeat the exchange: Dawlish did not know whether to be surprised or pleased when he heard 'Kensington, London'.

He thought of the curly-headed Dr Bingham, at Appleton Mansions.

Chapter 11

Telephone Tactics

Fanessa held the line for a long time.

Dawlish looked idly through the papers he had taken from the man's pockets, and then those of the gunman's. Except for the name 'Carter' on the envelopes of several letters, he found nothing of interest. In Fanessa's case, one from a theatrical agent confirmed a booking at a south country music hall the following week. Vaguely, Dawlish remembered hearing the name 'Fanessa' before, but could not recall it to mind in any definite connection.

At the telephone, Fanessa began to speak.

'Give me the Chief, quickly. Quickly.'

Dawlish waited a minute, and then took two strides across the room, and removed the instrument from Fanessa's hand.

Fanessa made an ineffectual attempt to retain it. Dawlish spread out his left hand, placed it on Fanessa's chest and pushed the man back against the wall, pinning him there as he said in friendly fashion:

'Why hallo, Chief. How are you?'

A sharp voice said in surprise: 'Who is that? Fanessa – '

'Fanessa is listening in, Chief,' Dawlish assured the other with relish. 'But he hasn't had too pleasant a time, and I'm speaking for him. My name is Dawlish,' he added. 'You may have heard of it. . . . No, don't ring off, or Fanessa will spend the night in jail.'

There was a long pause before the sharp voice said: 'What do you want?'

'Fair exchanges, nothing more,' said Dawlish chattily. 'Amelia returned in first-class condition, or Fanessa and his little friend with the gun will be delivered up to the police. Quite simple.'

'I know nothing about any Amelia,' snapped the other.

Apart from the fact that it was definitely not Bingham's there was nothing to give Dawlish any information in the voice itself. He imagined it to be that of an oldish man –

certainly it was not a young voice – and there was an incisive note about it which Dawlish respected.

'Strange,' said Dawlish. 'Fanessa gave me the impression that you did. Still, my original offer still stands. Unless Amelia Shortt returns to Clay House by six o'clock this evening, Fanessa and his little friend will go to the nearest police station where, you can believe me, there will be some rather pointed questions asked. Is that clear?'

'You are talking nonsense!' snapped the other.

'Well, perhaps,' said Dawlish. 'I'm often told that I do. Remember, by six o'clock this evening. Oh, yes – and un-harmed. Virtue unblemished, innocence untarnished and all the usual things.'

'I have no idea what you are talking about,' snapped the other.

'Well, that's too bad for Fanessa,' said Dawlish. 'But just in case it should strike a chord in your memory before six o'clock, provided Amelia arrives at Clay House, Fanessa and his boy friend may go free. Go free, I said, not stay free. Get it?'

'I have never heard such drivel in all my life!'

'What an intriguing life you must have led,' said Dawlish brightly. 'Oh, by the way, what's your number?

The man said: 'Kensington one-eight – *damn* you!' he added on an explosive note, and then the receiver banged down, its reverberations making unpleasant discord in Dawlish's ears.

Dawlish smiled gently to himself, replaced the receiver, and regarded Fanessa reflectively.

'Not a very friendly soul, the Chief,' he said regretfully. 'I suppose he's better when you get to know him.'

'What – what did he say?' demanded Fanessa thickly.

'He denied knowing you,' said Dawlish sadly. 'That's a bad habit with some employers, they don't like accepting responsibility for their less successful workmen. Still, he may change his mind. You heard the offer I made to him.'

'Damn you!' muttered Fanessa, and turned away.

Dawlish also turned.

Jones was no longer sitting in his chair in an attitude of utter dejection, but was standing in front of Posslethwaite. His eyes were shining, and his whole face showed a happiness and contentment Dawlish had not seen before.

'Why, hallo,' said Dawlish. 'Better?'

'We were in time!' exclaimed Jones, turning swiftly. 'We were in time, Major Dawlish, he will be all right now!'

'Good,' said Dawlish. 'On the whole we haven't done too badly.' He smiled at Posslethwaite who was gaining strength with every minute.

'Does the name Fanessa mean anything to you?'

'It does, indeed, Dawlish.'

'So, we've plenty to discuss.'

'Plenty is right,' admitted the man in the invalid chair.

'But before we go on to that,' said Dawlish, 'we have to decide what to do now. There is the chance, you know, that Fanessa's Chief might send a reinforcement to help him. Faced with such an ultimatum it is probably what I would do myself.'

'Ah see what you mean,' said Posslethwaite. 'But we can go from here whenever you like, Dawlish.'

'Excellent. Let's have a drink on it,' said Dawlish heartily. 'Not that this isn't a jolly place. Nice rooms and plenty of window space, you know, but perhaps we'd feel a little more comfortable if we were somewhere else for the time being. Don't you agree?'

'Ah do an' all,' said Posslethwaite emphatically. 'Ah'll be reet enough to move in less than half-an-hour – if Jones will let me,' he added with a ruminative smile.

Jones, happily bouncing in with a tray of bottles and glasses, stipulated only that Posslethwaite should not move for at least another twenty minutes.

Dawlish accepted a drink with pleasure, lit a cigarette, and asked thoughtfully:

'Do you run to a car?'

'We have one, yes,' said Jones quickly.

'If you're asking what we'll do with them,' said Posslethwaite with a nod towards the two captives, 'don't worry yourself. We can take them in an ambulance – this is a private nursing home, or had you forgotten that?'

'I had indeed,' admitted Dawlish.

'Telephone for Fowler,' said Posslethwaite to Jones.

Jones did so, making arrangements for the ambulance to be outside at four o'clock.

Posslethwaite said sharply: 'Put them to sleep, Jones.'

By 'them' it was obvious that he meant the prisoners. Fanessa looked up with a start, while the little gunman eased himself to one side and then stopped, gasping with pain.

Both of them looked a mess, but it did not occur to Dawlish until then that there might be a more serious injury. He stepped over to the gunman, conscious of Jones's disapproving eye, and ran a hand lightly over him. He found that there was a fracture in the right leg, and was amazed still further at the strength that had been in Jones's wild onslaught. Whether Jones liked it or not the leg had to be set: he said so, briefly. Jones looked questioningly at Posslethwaite.

'Aye, get on wi' it,' said Posslethwaite.

There was no doubt that the little man was accomplished at such work. Adroitly, if without compassion, a splint was produced and the leg set before the ambulance arrived.

Whatever drug was used in the hypodermic syringe, it worked very quickly. Inside a minute both men were unconscious.

'It won't hurt them, Major, they won't even have a morning-after. Don't worry yourself about them.' His eyes were bright as he looked at Dawlish. 'Ah won't be sorry to have a little chinwag wi' you.'

'Nor me with you,' said Dawlish, and meant it.

When the ambulance arrived, two men appeared bearing folded stretchers and blankets. In a surprisingly short time Fanessa and Carter were on their way downstairs.

Posslethwaite was the next to go, a long four-handled piece of wood being thrust beneath the invalid chair. It held securely, and the invalid was carried down without jolting and without great difficulty.

Dawlish and Jones climbed in beside him.

Smoothly and calmly the ambulance moved off. Dawlish had no idea where they were going. He was confident enough that Posslethwaite had everything arranged and was fully prepared against such an eventuality.

They stopped at last outside a house very similar to that in Mere Street, and Dawlish, glad to be out of the cramped interior of the ambulance, stepped down and stretched his legs. He stayed on the pavement, looking about him. It was very quiet, deceptively so. Posslethwaite was brought out of the ambulance and his chair carried into the house. Dawlish caught a glimpse of a white-clad nurse, and more than a whiff of antiseptics.

It was after the front door had closed behind him that he saw Dr Claude Bingham.

Chapter 12

Posslethwaite Explains A Little

Dawlish was the first to recover.

He was standing at the foot of the stairs, and Posslethwaite, followed by Jones, was being carried upwards by the silent attendants. The hall itself was empty except for Dawlish and Bingham.

'Hallo,' said Dawlish mildly. 'Did you have a good journey?'

'D-D-Dawlish!' gasped Bingham.

'Right first time,' said Dawlish admiringly.

'D-D-Dawlish!' gasped Bingham again, incredulously.

'Yes, you've said so once,' said Dawlish a little testily.

'H-How did you get here?'

'In an ambulance,' said Dawlish promptly. 'Not the most comfortable means of transport, but it served all right.'

Before he could go on, Jones came tripping down the stairs, his face alive with pleasure. He paused in front of Dawlish and began to introduce the two men, then broke off with an exclamation.

'Ah! But how absurd of me, of course you know each other. Dr Bingham probably didn't expect to see you, Major Dawlish, only a very favoured few are allowed here. Eh, Doctor?' He looked positively roguish. 'But Major Dawlish has proved himself our very good friend, our *very* good friend. Major, Mr Posslethwaite would be delighted to see you upstairs, if – '

'Just a moment,' said Dawlish, and moved to the front door.

'But – ' began Jones.

'I won't be long,' promised Dawlish.

Leaving both men staring after him he stepped into the street. A long terrace of tall houses stretched on either side. He strode towards the right.

The presence of Bingham was one of the many things

which would need explanation, Dawlish knew, but what had suddenly occurred to him was that Ted Beresford was sure to be fairly close at hand. Scanning every yard of the way, Dawlish reached the porch of a nearby house. In it a khaki-clad figure was standing with its back towards him.

Dawlish chuckled aloud, and called: 'Want some help, Ted?'

Beresford, for it was he, turned about in the narrow confines of the porch, startled at first and then beaming, his ugly face transformed, as always, by his smile.

'Nicely done,' said Dawlish, 'a blind man couldn't possibly have seen you, Ted!'

'One does one's best,' said Beresford primly, his grin widening. 'The thing is, Bingham's up here.'

'I've seen him,' said Dawlish.

Beresford's eyebrows shot up.

'You are the little early bird, aren't you?'

'Nice to be appreciated,' said Dawlish cheerfully. 'What did you do with Hubbard?'

'Left him at the flat, kicking his heels, bemoaning his fate, and cursing me. I think he thinks that we're conspiring to keep him out of the show. Actually he won't be so bad, but I've some really first class news for you.'

'And that is?'

'None other than Timothy will be at the Grand Hotel at half-past five.'

Dawlish's eyes lit up.

'Here, in Manchester, d'you mean?'

'In the city of Manchester itself,' Beresford assured him. 'The way things are going I thought it would be worthwhile seeing if he could get a few days off, so I telephoned his unit. Congratulations, please.'

'Congratulations indeed,' said Dawlish heartily. 'I think you'd better meet him there, Ted, and then bring him along to this place. 41 – ' He looked at a nameplate on the wall of the corner house, and added: 'King's Road. A nursing home, and at the moment they all love me like a brother. What brought Bingham up here? Any ideas?'

'None at all. I went with Hub to Appleton Mansions, and after about ten minutes Bingham went along to his other surgery. He was there for half-an-hour, and came out carrying a suitcase. We went after him, and he landed at Euston. I told Hub to go back, and caught the same train as Bingham.

73

I don't think he knows that I'm here.'

'Nice work all round,' said Dawlish appreciatively. 'You'd better ring Hubbard at the flat and ask him to go along to Clay House. He should be there by a quarter to six at the latest. If Amelia turns up he's to stick very close to her. Tell him she isn't to leave the place until we get back.'

Beresford exclaimed: 'Amelia!'

'Yes. Things have moved somewhat, and I'm staking Amelia against a music-hall artiste named Fanessa.' Dawlish looked interrogatively at his friend. 'Does it mean anything?'

Beresford pondered at some length, and then shook his head.

'I wonder if it would be wise to have a word with Trivett about this, Ted? Just murmur "Fanessa" into his ear, and tell him that the man might be involved – underlining the might.'

'Right.'

'Wait a minute,' said Dawlish, thoughtfully. 'I don't know that we want Bill to know where we are at this moment. Give the message to Hubbard, and ask him to pass it on. Hubbard hasn't any idea of where we are, as far as Trivett's concerned. I don't think there's anything else, but I'm glad you're around.'

'Anything else?'

'It might be an idea to watch Mere Street. Go there after you've got the telephoning done, and take Tim with you. If you spend half-an-hour there, you should be back here by half-past six or so. All clear?'

'Crystal clear,' Beresford assured him.

'Good man,' said Dawlish with feeling. He was about to turn away when he thought of Felicity, who would be waiting for news from him. 'I wonder if we should ask Fel to go to Clay House?' he mused aloud. 'She won't want to be kept out of this any longer. I had hoped to look in and collect her this evening, but there may not be time. Yes, do that – give her a ring too.'

'And on what other subject would you like to change your mind?' demanded Beresford.

'I'll let you know,' said Dawlish with mock seriousness. 'Give Tim my love!'

Walking back towards the nursing home, he mused with great contentment. Tim Jeremy was as useful as Ted Beresford; he would be a tower of strength in the next few days. And, thought Dawlish, there was going to be plenty for all of them to do, for the affair had little more than started as far as he could see. The sooner he learned what Posslethwaite was prepared to tell him the better he would be pleased. But the situation had, in any case, improved very much for the better. With Ted and Tim at hand everything was covered for the immediate future, so that he could concentrate on Posslethwaite and Fanessa.

He wished he knew why the name was so vaguely familiar to him.

Jones was standing by the open front door, moving from one foot to another agitatedly: and as Dawlish appeared again, Bingham's fair, curly head disappeared behind a curtain.

'*Major* Dawlish!' exclaimed Jones explosively. 'I don't know what Mr Posslethwaite will say, you have kept him waiting for nearly twenty-five minutes.' He looked accusingly into Dawlish's lazy eyes, then turned abruptly to lead the way upstairs.

Outside a door on the first landing, Jones stopped and rested a hand lightly on Dawlish's forearm.

'Major Dawlish,' he said humbly, 'please do forgive me for my extremely inappropriate comments just now. I am a little distraught, and I have a great regard for Mr Posslethwaite, as doubtless you will have perceived. I am deeply appreciative of your invaluable assistance. I doubt whether we would have been alive had you not acted with such superb courage and presence of mind.'

Dawlish resisted a temptation to ruffle the little man's thin, mousy hair.

'Forgiven, Jones,' he said, amiably.

'I knew you would understand, Major Dawlish. What a wonderful thing, the faculty of understanding the faults and shortcomings of other, lesser men.' He turned quickly, and tapped on the door.

They found Posslethwaite sitting in his chair by the window.

By some queer coincidence the room was built so that the sun came through the window about the same angle as it had at the Mere Street house, half-blinding Dawlish, so that he saw Posslethwaite only as a vague, blurred figure, not even seeing his smile. What he glimpsed of the room in the first moment made it seem as if they were back in Mere Street, for the chairs and the desk were in similar positions and were of similar style.

The dominating figure here, as there, was Posslethwaite.

'I'm sorry I'm late,' he said: and the odd thing was that he meant it.

'Ah wouldn't worry about that, Major, you've a right to what time Ah have left. Ah'm not forgetting that you saved our bacon at yon place.' Posslethwaite nodded towards the window. 'But Ah'm greatly concerned to hear that the police might be near at hand, greatly concerned. Can you prevent them from becoming too curious?'

Dawlish raised one eyebrow.

'If they were here, I couldn't.'

Posslethwaite frowned.

Dawlish leaned forward.

'The police have already heard of Mere Street. They told me on the telephone this morning that it was a private house, occupied by a man who had been living there for twenty years. The general idea was that it was an address picked at random so that I should visit it, and then be disappointed,' he added. 'Apart from that, no police.'

Jones squeaked: 'But I distinctly heard you tell – '

'Hold your tongue,' said Posslethwaite good-humouredly, and he gave a deep and pleasant chuckle which made Dawlish warm to him.

'Ah've come to believe that the one thing we mustn't do in this affair is to under-rate Major Dawlish,' he continued with relish. 'Happen he looks a fool at times, but it's no more than looks.'

'Nice of you,' murmured Dawlish.

'You'll want a man to call a spade a spade, or Ah'll be reet disappointed in you,' said Posslethwaite. 'Give me a cigarette, Jones, please.' He waited until Jones had struck a match for him, and then said: 'Now who'll start the talking, Major?'

'I hope, you,' said Dawlish.

'Aye. You've the reet to expect it, an' all,' said Posslethwaite. 'And you aren't a man who'll want a lot of words, you'll see through most of it when Ah tell you the main points.'

'I'll try,' said Dawlish.

'Here's one,' said Posslethwaite, giving the impression

that he was being wholly frank. 'The reason for it all, Dawlish, or' – he paused – 'one of the reasons, and the only one we know so far.'

'Yes?' Dawlish said mildly.

'Do you know what Dr Shortt was working on?' Posslethwaite surprised him with the question.

'Vaguely,' said Dawlish.

'Ah,' said Posslethwaite. 'Happen you'll know that he's trying to improve the lot of poor unfortunate folk who've been turned mad or dull-witted by what's happened to them.'

'Yes,' said Dawlish. 'I'd gathered that.'

'It's all you need to know,' said Posslethwaite.

Dawlish did not interrupt, even when the other man drew at his cigarette and eyed him steadily for several minutes. Jones was so quiet that he might not have been there. Dawlish's earlier impression that Posslethwaite was a man of power and of intellect grew apace. It was a fact that there emanated from the man in the wheelchair an impression of great strength and power.

'Ah'm one he's practised on,' said Posslethwaite at last.

Dawlish was startled into an exclamation.

'Ah don't give you the impression of being a man wi' a brain that won't work, Ah hope,' said the other drily. 'But until a month ago Ah hadn't the sense of a child of fower. Jones had to do my thinking for me,' he added, sending a humorous glance across the room. 'Isn't that so, Jones?'

'No, no, no!' exclaimed Jones. 'I only helped to nurse you back to health, sir, no more than that!'

Dawlish thought that he understood something of the bond between these two men. He needed no more telling that Posslethwaite had been sick almost to death – and, worse, to madness. Shortt had 'experimented'. Jones had helped in the treatment.

'Ah was an early patient, Dawlish, and Dr Shortt had not evolved some of the treatment he has now. It was touch and go, Ah reckon, whether Ah died or not, but between them they kept me alive, and through me they found improvements, so that there is a greater chance now for men and women to recover. Ah want to live to see such a recovery, Dawlish, but apart from that Ah care little what happens to me. It falls to few men to know that they have been a means of saving the minds of thousands.'

77

After a pause, Posslethwaite went on:

'But Ah discovered all was not well wi' the doctor, Dawlish. Ah discovered he was being victimised. More than that, I discovered him to be in mortal danger. Ah mean it,' added Posslethwaite very softly. 'Ah mean it if it's the last words Ah speak. And – ' Posslethwaite's voice strengthened, there was a fierce undertone to it, his hands were clenched and the expression in his eyes told Dawlish that every fibre in his being throbbed with the sincerity of what he said. 'And,' repeated Posslethwaite, 'Shortt is too great a man to be allowed to die. Ah care nowt for your law, nowt for your police and your Home Office. Shortt must be saved and Ah'll save him if Ah'm spared.'

Dawlish, oddly affected, nodded.

'Happen the man has broken the law,' went on Posslethwaite. 'So have most of us, Major; he's no exception. Such a man must be allowed to live his own way. But there are other forces, and in the course of his work Shortt had met them. Ah'll be as simple as Ah can, Dawlish. Shortt has other patients far more important than Ah myself. Brilliant men, brilliant minds. One of them – Ah've no reet t'tell you his name now – is wanted very much indeed by Fanessa and those murdering scoundrels who work wi' him.'

Dawlish said, very slowly: 'I see.'

'Ah should think you do,' said Posslethwaite. 'Ah'm telling you, Major, that Shortt is afraid that the swine will give information about some things he has done to the police, and knowing the police they would arrest him and keep him away from his laboratory, away from his patients – damned fools that they are! They'd have their petty justice when a man is on the threshold of a new life, a new life for old and broken ones, Major. Not if Ah know it,' added Posslethwaite grimly. 'That's why his daughter, Bingham and myself are anxious not to have the police advised, why Ah've taken great chances. They've kidnapped Shortt all right – but they'll not kill him. Ah'm telling you they'll give him a laboratory and patients and all he needs, to continue his work.'

'Yes,' said Dawlish thinly.

'But they've other ways of getting what they want,' said Posslethwaite. 'They might persuade him by injuring Amelia, they might – but that doesn't matter now. Major, *this* is what matters. One of Shortt's patients is badly wanted by

Fanessa's employer. A brilliant man, on the way to recovery. He's hidden away where no one can get to him. Fanessa wanted me to give him the address. You see, Major, Ah'm the only one who knows it, except Jones. Ah wouldn't trust Shortt with it. And what we're fighting for is the safety of that patient and the release of Shortt and his daughter, without any interference from the police. That's where we want your help, and Ah'm hoping we shall have it.'

Chapter 13

Frolics At Mere Street

Dawlish nodded slowly, but did not immediately answer. He was impressed by Posslethwaite's story, and felt little doubt of its genuineness. There was in it some explanation of the passionate devotion which Jones showed towards the invalid, for it was clear that Jones had helped to nurse a man back from the limbo of the lost. Yet there were reservations even in what he had been told, and these he considered as he regarded Posslethwaite steadily.

First, the reason for Shortt's fear of the police; that was a powerful influence in the affair. Posslethwaite had admitted that the doctor had committed some offence which would justify the police in arresting him on a charge which Posslethwaite obviously considered would be judged pretty severely.

Dawlish felt that what Posslethwaite had told him explained Amelia's unusual method of approach, while giving some indication of the reason why she had rejoiced on the telephone with Bingham and allowed it to be thought that Shortt was worried by a blackmailer. Bingham had stuck to the same story. The truth, thought Dawlish, was that Shortt was being victimised by Fanessa's 'Chief' for the reason which Posslethwaite had given him, and Amelia and Bingham had been desperately anxious not to say anything which might prejudice Dawlish against the research man.

But Posslethwaite had made a second and perhaps more important reservation by withholding the name of the man whom Fanessa and his associates so badly wanted to detain. A 'patient of Shortt's' was too vague, but that had been deliberate and he doubted whether Posslethwaite would go further at the moment.

The north-countryman eyed him with that same grim humour which he had revealed so often.

'Well, Major?' he said at last.

Dawlish rubbed his nose.

'There are complications, aren't there?' he said mildly. 'For one thing, Kibb's murder. You've heard of that, I take it?'

'Aye.'

'The police aren't fools,' said Dawlish. 'I think they'll find out who killed Kibb, and that means that they'll get pretty close to the heart of the trouble. If they do that, the whole story will come out. Nothing you or I do can prevent it.'

'*If* they get to the heart of the trouble I'll agree with you,' conceded Posslethwaite, 'but I doubt whether it will be as easy for the police as you think.'

'Probably you don't know them as well as I do,' mused Dawlish. 'However, that's by the way. There are other things – the motives. Why do they want Shortt's patient?'

'Ah can't tell you,' said Posslethwaite deliberately.

'Do you know?' asked Dawlish.

'Ah do,' said Posslethwaite.

'I don't know whether you're wise to keep it back,' Dawlish said thoughtfully. 'I have to be governed by certain obvious principles, you know. I'm a member of His Majesty's Forces, and if this business should be in any way connected with the war, any part I play would have to be official.'

'Official?' Posslethwaite frowned.

Dawlish said carefully: 'I can't touch anything which might, even remotely, be connected with espionage without informing my superiors and getting their ruling.'

'No,' said Posslethwaite. 'But I don't know of anything to suggest that it is, Dawlish. Why should you think it might be?'

'Fanessa might be an Italian.'

It was clear enough to Dawlish that he had startled Posslethwaite, and equally clear that Jones was as surprised, for the little man uttered another excited cascade of clucking noises, and earned a swift glance of disapproval from Posslethwaite. The north-countryman said sharply:

'If you were officially interested, what would it mean?'

'Well, several things.' Dawlish deliberated. 'It need not mean that I would have to take the police into my confidence. It could even strengthen my hand against them. If the Powers That Be ruled that I was to have *carte blanche*, then *carte blanche* it would be. I could also have at my disposal a number of capable men, and could call on the police for a variety of purposes. That of course would give me ample time to concentrate on the problem. They're the advantages.'

'Aye,' said Posslethwaite drily. 'Ah'm waiting for the disadvantages.'

Dawlish smiled.

'Well, eventually we'd find the truth. Fanessa's leaders, Shortt's motives for secrecy, yours, Bingham's and Amelia's. My C.O. might not agree with you that whatever Shortt had done in the past should be kept away from the police. Mind you,' he added carefully, 'it's no more than "might not". It's no part of his business or mine to delve into cupboards, we've often uncovered skeletons and covered them up again. But neither my C.O. nor I could promise anything.' He smoothed the back of his head, and then smiled more widely. 'I did say complications! And there's one more, which you mightn't like too much. Having discovered so much I don't see that I can back out. And if I don't back out but go on and discover something connected with espionage, I must report. Pretty awkward, isn't it?'

Posslethwaite deliberated for some time, then said:

'Ah don't know that it is, Dawlish. If there's any connection with the Nazis then it must be found out, we can't hide that. Ah'll take the chance wi' you.'

'Well put,' smiled Dawlish, with genuine relief.

'And now what's to do with Fanessa and the other man?' asked Posslethwaite, obviously anxious to change the subject. 'Is there any chance of getting Amelia back?'

'A fair one, I'd say,' said Dawlish, and explained briefly what arrangements he had made to find out whether Amelia returned. Then slowly: 'I didn't ask for Shortt in exchange for Fanessa, because I don't think his boy-friend would think him worth the exchange. Shortt is his golden egg, at the moment. Yes?'

'There's no doubt about that,' said Posslethwaite. 'Ah think you were wise, Dawlish. As Ah said before Ah'm not worried that they'll do owt to injure Shortt, but Ah think they would have been less careful of Amelia. There isn't much we can do at this stage, is there?'

'No,' admitted Dawlish. 'We can get one or two things ready, though. Fanessa, for instance, will have to be released if Amelia returns, and – '

'Released! Fanessa!' Jones jumped to his feet and rushed forward, both hands held high. 'What absurdity is this! We have him, now we shall keep him! You would not be such a fool as to release him!'

Dawlish eyed him mildly.

'We have to stick to certain rules even in a show like this, Jones. If we don't do our share we'd have no possible foundation for expecting to do a deal with Fanessa's chief on something else, when a little mild deception might be more important. Fanessa doesn't matter all that much,' he added carelessly. 'A cog in the wheel, but not irreplaceable. Apart from that' – he smiled very gently – 'he would not go unescorted. I would follow him, or someone else could who knows his way about. Fanessa might lead us to many unexpected places and people of interest. You see, Jones?'

'The man is dangerous,' muttered Jones.

'Don't be daft, man,' said Posslethwaite, 'it's clear enough to all that the Major is reet.'

Dawlish smiled a little, satisfied that Posslethwaite meant what he said and that Jones would not try to sabotage any arrangements. Carter, he knew, would have to stay at the nursing home for some time, at least until he was able to walk on his own, but that was not a point of any importance.

'We can get more out of Fanessa later by making a fair exchange now,' he suggested.

'But how do you know they will release Amelia?' demanded Jones with a triumphant air.

Dawlish shrugged.

'If they don't, we have to make new plans, but I fancy they will. Now – there's Bingham.'

'Yes,' said Posslethwaite.

'He told me a story last night which I thought was true in the main,' said Dawlish, 'and the point of importance was that he and Shortt had quarrelled. What is he doing here?'

Posslethwaite said: 'Ah sent for him. He was one of Shortt's assistants, and knows as much about Shortt's methods as any man. There's a patient here who needs urgent attention, and Shortt would have been up here today to see him. As he can't come, someone else had to. Major, Ah'll make this thing clear. Ah'm interested *only* in Shortt's work, in its results, in giving men a new chance to live. Ah'd use the devil himself if Ah thought it necessary. Bingham and Shortt did quarrel. Bingham's a self-opinionated young pup, but he's a clever doctor. Does that answer your question?'

'Yes,' said Dawlish. 'But here's another. What's the connection between Bingham and Amelia?'

He was startled by the effect of his words.

Posslethwaite frowned, his brows grew dark, his eyes stormy. His hands gripped the sides of his chair and the whole expression of his face altered. It was in that moment that Dawlish realised that Posslethwaite was in love with Amelia Shortt. It was a blinding revelation, one which put him momentarily off his balance, yet prepared him for Posslethwaite's rough:

'The fool thinks she'll marry him.'

Deliberately obtuse, Dawlish said: 'And will she?'

'She's got more sense,' growled Posslethwaite. 'She wouldn't have a thing to do with him if she didn't know that one day Shortt will want his help again. She's a clever lass, Amelia, she had him on a piece of string and she'll keep him there as long as there's a chance of him doing some good. And that's enough about Bingham, Major.'

Nothing Posslethwaite had said on that subject differed with what Dawlish had already been told. Certainly what he knew of Amelia suggested that she would be quite heartless enough to inveigle Bingham with half-promises until she had obtained what she wanted from him. She would have no regard at all for Bingham's feelings.

Would she have for Posslethwaite's?

Dawlish thought it unlikely, and believed that Posslethwaite was fully aware of that. He did not go on with the subject, however, but did establish several other factors of interest. Amongst them that Posslethwaite was a research scientist of some renown who had been working in conjunction with Shortt for years, Jones being his chief assistant. Neither Posslethwaite nor Jones gave any hint as to the reason for Posslethwaite's mental collapse; but there had been one, and Shortt had succoured him.

If Dawlish was not wholly satisfied, he had obtained as much satisfaction as he could reasonably expect. Many of the minor problems had solved themselves, mysteries were no longer mysteries. Much depended on his ability to keep a safe check on Fanessa.

It was then that he remembered that he had forgotten to get Fanessa's telephone number from the Exchange, and decided that the most effective way of doing this was to ring up from the Mere Street house. He said abruptly:

'Posslethwaite, you expected trouble at Mere Street, didn't you?'

'Ah did,' admitted Posslethwaite. 'You must know why, Major. Ah didn't give you the Mere Street address by telegram, *they* did. They knew you were busy wi' us, and they thought they could catch us all together if they got you to come there. Fanessa thought he had succeeded, and but for the way you acted he would have done.'

Dawlish smiled.

'As I see it, whoever pretended to telegraph me did telegraph you. They lured me into coming here, wired you to make sure you waited there expecting me. On the whole, they're thorough. I don't think Fanessa is anything like clever enough to handle the whole thing alone.'

'Ah think you're right,' agreed Posslethwaite. 'But Ah'm not so sure that you're right to go to Mere Street now.'

Dawlish smiled.

'It's safe enough,' he said. 'There'll be others there.'

He did not say whom he expected to find at Mere Street, other than Ted Beresford and Tim Jeremy. He took a taxi to a nearby avenue and walked the rest of the way.

Turning the corner, he stood amazed. The street as he remembered it, so quiet and dull, was now filled with a jostling crowd. He was thankful to see the stalwart figure of Ted Beresford, and inched towards him.

Chapter 14

Pitiful Little Man

Strange noises were coming from Number 81, encouraged by cries and cat-calls from a jeering audience.

'What the hell's going on?' he demanded.

Beresford looked round quickly, his face grim.

'Some crazy frolic, if you can judge from appearances, and the police aren't helping much. Tim's inside.'

Three policemen were hammering on the front door, while another two were running a ladder up to one of the upper windows.

At one of them a man was capering. Now and again he disappeared, then came back again with a bugle, which he put to his lips. A single piercing note cut through the discord. Again, and yet again. Tired of it at last, the man dropped the bugle and continued his crazy miming; then lifted a pair of cymbals and crashed them together.

He was a red-faced man, naked from the waist upwards except for some gaily-coloured ribbons tied about his neck. The grotesque contortions of his face struck a chill note into Dawlish, who was quite sure that this man was mad; but the madness was suited to the humour of the crowd, which roared with laughter, young and old alike.

One of the policemen began to mount the ladder, and Dawlish admired his singleness of purpose. The creature at the window looked out, saw a steel helmet and dived out of sight again. The crowd began to roar for him.

'Coom back, there!'

'Tha scared o' a uniform, tha art!'

'Give us another tune, mister!'

The central actor in the tragi-comedy of 81, Mere Street reappeared with the suddenness of Punch, and brought forth another roar of laughter from his audience. The policeman was halfway up to the window, and the man looked down. He had the bugle in his hand, but instead of blowing on it, he gripped it at the thin end and used it as a club. It cracked against the steel helmet, giving off a tinny sound which brought another roar of laughter.

Dawlish said abruptly: 'Come on, Ted.'

Together they inched their way to the front of the house, as the policeman came stumbling blindly down the ladder. Without asking permission, Dawlish and Beresford moved it to the next window, and Dawlish began to climb.

'Look out, lad!' roared the crowd to the man above.

'T'other window, be careful!'

Damned fools, thought Dawlish. He lost no time in reaching the window ledge, with Beresford holding the ladder steady, but a shout of delight told him that the man at the other window had disappeared; obviously the crowd thought he was changing his venue.

He was.

From the window at the top of the ladder Dawlish saw the man rushing towards him, stark naked except for the ribbons fluttering about his neck. Dawlish bent his arm and cracked his elbow through the glass. Pieces fell inwards, and the crazed man stopped for a moment. But only for a moment, for as Dawlish stepped through he rushed at him with the bugle upraised and began to belabour him about the head and shoulders. Dawlish, knowing there was only one way of silencing him, doubled his fists and brought them against the other's chin with an upper-cut.

Only the one punch was needed.

The man did not lose consciousness, but backed away, hurt and frightened.

The crowd was roaring for another act.

Dawlish was heedless of them, but worried, for there was no sign of Tim Jeremy. For the moment he had his work cut out to hold the madman fast, but in a few seconds Ted appeared at the window, then called down to the police. In a few minutes the little naked man – for he was not much larger than Jones – was laying quietly on a bed in a nearby room.

The police were asking questions, too many questions.

Dawlish kept his patience, and persuaded them that the first thing to do was to search the place. He went to room after room but found no one there, and no sign at all of Tim Jeremy.

But in the room where Dawlish had seen Posslethwaite

for the first time there was evidence enough of a recent visitation. Papers were thrown everywhere, some had been burnt, others were still smouldering in the grate. Dawlish wondered whether it was the work of the little man now so pitifully helpless on the bed, then set the thoughts aside.

A doctor had been urgently sent for. On his authority the crazed man was taken in an ambulance to hospital – a small emergency hospital on the outskirts of the city, Dawlish was told. He made a note of it so that Posslethwaite would know where the man was, and then contrived to get away from the house.

The crowd, robbed of its sensation, had dispersed. Only a few stragglers remained, and none of them appeared to be particularly interested in Dawlish or Beresford.

Dawlish told the cabby to drive to King's Road, and then settled back grimly.

'Just what happened?'

'I don't really know,' admitted Beresford. 'There was no one there when we arrived, and we tossed up who should knock at the door and try to get in. Tim won. I didn't expect much, and thought he would come out after making the usual apologies for a mistake, but – well, he didn't. I waited ten minutes, and was about to follow him up when I heard the door being locked. Then I went round the back, but there was no way in. When I got to the front again that poor little beggar was at the window. Someone had switched on the radio, and – ' Beresford shrugged. 'You can fill in the details yourself.'

'Yes,' said Dawlish thoughtfully. 'And no sign at all of Tim?'

'None at all,' said Beresford helplessly.

For the first time a glimmer of a smile entered Dawlish's eyes, and he spoke more lightly.

'It looks to me as if Tim discovered that there was much amiss, and that there were others than the patient there. He probably followed them after they'd set fire to the papers. Odd, but it might be useful in the long run.'

Beresford said: 'Tim could have been put out of action.'

'Well, yes,' admitted Dawlish, 'but if he had been I think we'd have found him. Whoever was there certainly went out the back way, and from what I could see from the windows there wasn't much chance of getting a car close to the house. So they must have walked. Anyone who was being carried away would have been spotted pretty soon. And since our men – imaginary men,' he admitted, 'but I don't think there's much doubt that they are real enough – had to get away in a hurry, then they wouldn't have time to carry Tim with them, even if they had wanted to. On the whole I think he went of his own free will, and we'll be hearing from him soon.'

'Well, we'll hope so,' said Beresford, unusually pessimistic.

They reached the King's Road nursing home, to find that Posslethwaite was in the study, but Jones had been sent out on some errand. Posslethwaite heard the story, and as it grew towards its climax his frown deepened.

'There's nothing too bad for them, Major. The swine! Yon little fellow was a patient – Ah didn't tell you that they took one away from Mere Street a week ago. And they've returned him, this way. They've played on his mind, they've made him worse even than he was. The – '

He drew a deep breath, and Dawlish could understand what the man was feeling.

Posslethwaite went on slowly: 'And the papers – there isn't much doubt about them. We had records of the cases at Mere Street, Fanessa once threatened to destroy them all. Records of the cases, or the treatment, of the experiments – it's vandalism of the worst kind, there's nothing too black for them.'

'The only records?' Dawlish asked sharply.

'No, no,' said Posslethwaite testily. 'We have duplicates in several cases. It's just an effort to frighten us, Dawlish, a way of trying to make us give up the man they want. They told me, and they told Shortt, that they would ruin all his work and undo everything he had done unless he gave them their own way.'

'Nice people,' Dawlish said. 'Do you know any of them except Fanessa?'

'Ah do not,' said Posslethwaite decisively. 'Ah know none of them but the two you've met. What hospital did you say they'd take him to?'

Dawlish told him.

'We'll have to try to get him back here,' said Posslethwaite, who looked very tired. 'His name is Anstey – Professor Martin Anstey, specialist in malarial diseases. He was caught in France before the war, they took him to Germany

89

– God knows what they did to him.'

'How did Fanessa's chaps get hold of him?' asked Dawlish.

'He was well enough to walk,' said Posslethwaite, 'and went out with a male nurse. The nurse came back alone. Major, for weeks now they have been doing everything they possibly could to undermine our confidence. What fools we were to wait so long for you!'

Dawlish said slowly: 'Or the police, Posslethwaite.'

'We couldn't go to the police,' said Posslethwaite sharply. 'I've told you the reason. They – Fanessa – would have told the police what Shortt was doing before, and – ' He drew a deep breath. 'You'll have to believe that it's more important that Shortt is a free man than a convict.'

'Ye-es,' said Dawlish, dubiously.

Posslethwaite looked at him dully. Much of the power which emanated from the man had gone, his eyes were cloudy, there was no strength in his hands. Jones came in, looked at him for a moment, then swung round on Dawlish.

'What have you been doing to him? What have you been doing?'

The little man waited for no answer, but went to the back of Posslethwaite's chair and wheeled him out of the room.

Beresford looked at Dawlish with his eyebrows raised, and said gently: 'Odd place, Pat.'

'Odd is the word,' said Dawlish. 'I've known shows more violent than this, but I'm damned if I've known any as odd. I think Posslethwaite's right, there's a cold devilishness behind this thing, to victimise a man like Anstey is out of all normal crime, it's inhuman, it's – ' Dawlish stopped suddenly and looked at his friend, then went on slowly: 'The method is pure Nazi. Odd use of the word "pure",' he added with a crooked smile. 'The more I see of it the less I like it, and I'm going to report to Whitehead.'

'Good,' said Beresford.

Whitehead was their C.O. at Whitehall, and for him they had considerable regard and respect. Dawlish had little doubt that he would get authority to go further into the affair of Dr Shortt, and he felt more at ease in his mind when he reached this decision. He was looking up the times of trains when the telephone rang.

They both looked at it for a moment, and Beresford said: 'It can't be Tim.'

'No, and we didn't give Hubbard this number. So it isn't likely to be for us,' he added, but lifted the receiver and said: 'Hallo?'

A feminine voice answered him quickly. He did not really recognise it, although he had more than an idea whose it was.

'Is Posslethwaite there?' she asked urgently. 'Is – Who is that speaking?'

'My name's Dawlish,' said Dawlish quietly.

'Pat!' cried Amelia Shortt into the telephone. 'Pat, you wizard! I'm free, that's why I rang up to tell you. I'm at Clay House again!'

Chapter 15

In The Wake Of Fanessa

Amelia said a great number of other things, elation in her voice, but nothing to suggest that she had undergone an ordeal of any significance. She had wanted only to tell Dawlish that she was free, and to pass on a message from her captors. Dawlish appreciated her discretion, for she talked obscurely, allowing him to understand what she meant while making sure that no one who overheard the conversation could imagine what it was about. He was coming more and more to esteem Amelia's astuteness.

The message was, in effect, a threat to Dawlish if he failed to honour his side of the bargain.

He told Amelia that Felicity Deverall would probably be at Clay House that evening, then asked for a word with Hubbard, who was at Amelia's side. Nothing untoward had happened, Hubbard assured him, but he appeared delighted to be in sole charge of Amelia for the time being.

'And of Felicity,' Dawlish reminded him. 'Just stay there, Hub. Don't leave the grounds on any pretext. This business is deep, and you might run into trouble.'

'In this company, I'll stay,' said Hubbard, with deep satisfaction.

'Good man,' said Dawlish, and rang down.

The decision to get in touch with Whitehead coupled with the news of Amelia's safe return cheered him. He discovered Jones in an adjoining room, where Posslethwaite lay asleep in the wheelchair standing at the foot of the bed. Jones looked up, his eyes troubled.

'If I was too abrupt, Major Dawlish, I beg you to excuse me, but I am afraid – I am afraid that I am never really myself when anything happens to Mr Posslethwaite. I have served him for twenty years, you see. I have seen him enduring a living death, and have seen him recovering. He does not believe that his cure will last, or become complete, but it will. It must.'

'I hope so,' said Dawlish quietly. 'And don't worry about my sensibilities. You've some good news for him when he wakes up. Amelia Shortt is free.'

'She is? She *has* been released! Major Dawlish, it is little short of a miracle!'

'No miracle,' said Dawlish. 'Just a straightforward piece of barter, because Fanessa is now going free and I shall follow him.'

He half-expected Jones to raise a further protest, but the little man seemed quite content.

It proved that before he had been given another injection Posslethwaite had given Jones instructions about Anstey, and Jones was proposing to get in touch with the hospital immediately. Dawlish waited only long enough to get an even clearer idea of the type and nature of the patients at the King's Road nursing home.

Without exception they were men of science, Jones told him. For one reason or another they had collapsed, and, knowing Shortt's work in that particular field, had put themselves under his care while knowing that at this stage the treatment was little more than experimental.

'In this home,' Jones said impressively, 'there are some of the most brilliant medical and scientific brains of the country, Major Dawlish – indeed, of the world. If Dr Shortt is successful, and I believe he will be, the benefit he will have given to mankind will be incalculable, incalculable!'

Dawlish could not rid himself of a feeling that Posslethwaite and Jones were over-anxious to impress him with the value of Shortt's work; but he dismissed that as ungenerous. The trouble, he admitted, was that he had too much to think and brood about, and his mind was too confused for clarity. He wanted to cling to essentials, the main facts of the case, and those facts were less concerned with medical research than with Fanessa, the 'Chief', and the other actors in the drama.

Once they were dealt with, then the other angles could be pondered.

Fanessa had recovered from the drug which had sent him to sleep, and was in a small room on the top floor of the house, with Carter; Jones had told Dawlish that Carter would be unable to walk for at least a fortnight, and probably longer. The little man seemed quite resigned to this.

Fanessa's close-set eyes were fixed glitteringly on Dawlish

as the latter entered the room.

Carter, too, looked at him, but more placidly.

'You've been lucky,' Dawlish said. 'Your Chief must like you, Fanessa.'

Fanessa drew a deep breath and said harshly: 'The girl has been released?'

'She's been released,' agreed Dawlish, 'and you're as free as the air.' He beamed. 'Apologies to that entertaining man at Kensington one-eight whatever-it-was, won't you, because Carter is *hors de combat*.'

Carter said nothing, and Fanessa exclaimed: 'Will you free him when he recovers?'

'I wouldn't be surprised,' said Dawlish.

It did not occur to him that the affair would remain on the unsolved list after Carter was fit enough to walk, but he saw no point in saying no. His matter-of-factness obviously put Fanessa at ease. At first unbelieving, the man's eyes glowed. Once or twice as he went down the stairs he looked sideways at Dawlish, as if expecting to be told this was a trick, that Dawlish did not propose to let him go.

Dawlish saw from a clock in the hall that it was five minutes to eight when Fanessa left King's Road. Thirty seconds later he saw Beresford go ahead of the man who might be an Italian and whose name had such a familiar ring. Thirty seconds later still Dawlish hurried away, but he did not seriously expect the chase to last long that night.

Near the bus stop in the Avenue was a telephone kiosk. Fanessa hesitated, then pulled open the door and stepped inside. Dawlish, seeing Beresford fifty yards further along the road, stopped where he was, deciding to leave Beresford to follow the man. When Fanessa came out of the kiosk, he took his place.

He asked for trunks, and then spoke formally.

'This is the police speaking. A long-distance call was made from this box a few minutes ago. Will you give me the number, please?'

'Just a minute,' said the girl.

There followed a whispered consultation at the other end of the wire, and then a fresh voice, more incisive, asked him for his authority. Dawlish, expecting that, said:

'I need the number quickly, but if you're dubious, get it and telephone it immediately to Scotland Yard. That's Whitehall, London, 1212.'

'I know the number,' said the supervisor acidly. 'Who is the message for?'

'Give it to Superintendent William Trivett,' said Dawlish.

His evidence of *bona fides* was obviously taken for granted, for the supervisor gave him the number: it was, as he thought it would be, Kensington 18212. He toyed with the idea of putting a call through, then dismissed it as unworthy; instead, he waited for the next bus. Reaching the Grand Hotel, he arranged to meet Beresford there, or for the hotel receptionist to take a telephone message. He did not think it likely that Fanessa would leave Manchester that night, and certainly the man would not go until the night train. Dawlish had a drink at the bar, found a comfortable chair in the lounge and stretched himself in it luxuriously. As the minutes passed he wondered whether Fanessa had led Beresford a longer dance than either of them had expected. The whole business had its particular humour.

It was nine o'clock when he was told that a telephone message had been sent from a Captain Beresford to the effect that their mutual friend was staying at the Riall Hotel.

'The Riall,' mused Dawlish. 'Odd.'

It was the same name as the safe deposit where Posslethwaite had a box. It might, thought Dawlish, be no more than a coincidence, but at least it was interesting. He left the Grand and walked towards Piccadilly again, reaching the Riall within a few minutes. A smaller, and less pretentious hotel than the Grand, it was approached by a door between two shops. Only a glass sign, hanging above the entrance, gave any intimation that there was a hotel there.

Dawlish was about to step inside when he heard his name called.

He was startled, for he had not expected Beresford to be waiting outside, but turning, he saw that it was not Beresford but Jeremy. The relief which flooded him was proof of how much more anxiety he had felt for Timothy Jeremy than he had acknowledged.

He strode over to the tall, thin man who was waiting in a doorway.

'So here you are!'

Timothy Jeremy, who had left the Mere Street house in such peculiar circumstances beamed upon him. His voice, although low-pitched, was remarkably deep and seemed to boom about them.

'You've done some guesswork, I take it?'

'You followed the vandals from Mere Street?' suggested Dawlish.

'I did indeed. Two of them, and they came straight here. And Pat, Ted's gone in after another customer. I thought I'd better stay outside, they're pretty familiar with my dial by now.'

'They aren't exactly strangers to mine,' said Dawlish, 'but with a bit of luck they won't associate Ted with us. How long have you been about here?'

'Getting on for an hour,' said Jeremy, 'and I'm both hungry and thirsty.'

'You can say that again,' said Dawlish with feeling. 'You'd better nip off for a snack, and come back as soon as possible. I'll be here, and you can take over from me while I do likewise.'

Jeremy, nothing loath, went off in search of a restaurant while Dawlish strolled past the hotel. Almost the first thing which caught his eye was a fascia board next door declaring that it was the Riall Safe Deposit Company.

He was considering this when Beresford came out of the Riall Hotel. He came up to Dawlish at once, his expression baffled and a little anxious.

'Pat, I don't know what, but there's something odd about to happen, if it isn't already happening. I followed Fanessa here. There were three or four other people waiting in the lounge – it's a poky place – and he joined them. I don't know whether I've been spotted or not. They left the lounge one after the other, and went downstairs.'

Dawlish said sharply: 'Down?'

'That's what I said. I've never seen a more villainous bunch of rogues in all my natural. Dagoes to a man, or I'm no judge. So is the manager, a surly-looking beggar, and at least two of the staff. There's an atmosphere in there that I don't like at all. Though the hotel's practically empty, they're sending every prospective customer away, saying they're full up, and they're as jumpy as blazes.' He paused, and then added helplessly: 'Well, what?'

'*Downstairs!*' repeated Dawlish, and drew a deep breath. 'I shouldn't have let Tim go.'

'Tim?'

'He was waiting here, and I sent him off for a snack,' Dawlish explained. 'The crucial thing is this: Posslethwaite has something lodged at the Riall Safe Deposit.' Beresford stared at him blankly, and Dawlish went on: 'Downstairs. Next door.'

Beresford exclaimed: 'My oath, that's it!'

'It seems like it,' said Dawlish. 'The snag is, no police.'

'You can't do this on your own –' began Beresford.

'Needs must,' said Dawlish. 'Ready for some strong-arm stuff, Ted?'

Beresford's eyes kindled, and a passing policeman eyed them with not a little interest. Dawlish gripped Beresford's arm and led him to the door of the Riall Hotel.

A man, in a soiled dinner-jacket, looked up from behind a bureau window. Above his head was a notice reading: *No Rooms.*

Dawlish took two steps towards him, and the man snapped:

'Can't you read?'

'Oh, yes,' said Dawlish.

'Well, don't waste my time,' said the man harshly. 'I've been on my feet all day, and I've told your friend we've no rooms.'

Yes, thought Dawlish, Beresford was right, there was an atmosphere about this place, a strangeness evident in the almost frightened gaze of the man behind the window. The gloom, the absence of guests, all contrived to make it more noticeable.

The man snapped out again: 'I tell you we've no rooms, and no –'

'Food,' said Dawlish pleasantly enough, 'and you've been on your feet all day. It's certainly time you had a rest.' He stretched out his hand. Before the other could move away he gripped the fellow's wrist. There was a single gasp, less of pain than of surprise, and then Dawlish put his left hand over the other's mouth and nose. Beresford nipped round to the side of the bureau, opened the door, and approached their victim from behind.

He saw what Dawlish could not see: the man was trying to touch a knob in the floor behind the desk. Beresford hooked the leg away, while Dawlish said:

'If Posslethwaite were here he'd say put him to sleep.'

'Up to you,' said Beresford. He held his right hand above

the unfortunate victim's neck and brought it down sharply. The man gasped and sagged downwards. 'I haven't lost the knack,' Beresford murmured with satisfaction. 'He'll be out for five minutes.'

'Not long enough,' said Dawlish.

Together they bound the man's hands and feet, and Dawlish took a handkerchief from the pocket of the soiled dinner-jacket and stuffed it into its owner's mouth.

The thing which puzzled Dawlish most was that the building was still a public hotel and the door downstairs open. If there were plans afoot to break into the Safe Deposit – and he took it for granted that there were – why was the door left open? True, the man behind the bureau window had been there to dismiss all applicants for rooms, but it looked a risky procedure.

'There's more than a chance that someone else will be coming,' he said. 'And if there's nobody to attend to them, it might give rise to inquiries.'

'There must be someone else in the place,' Beresford said.

'And that someone else, if summoned, would immediately go to the desk and discover our little friend. We must find a more secluded hiding place.'

At the distant end of the lounge was a large settee. Dawlish lifted their victim and carried him to it. Beresford pulled it a couple of feet from the wall. Dawlish deposited his burden, and then the settee was pushed back into place. The whole operation took less than two minutes.

'Do you feel happier now?' Beresford asked briefly.

'Only slightly,' said Dawlish. 'Uncanny's the word. I don't like this place.' They reached the head of a flight of stairs. 'Is this where your johnnies went?'

'One at a time, and looking extremely furtive,' said Beresford. 'I've never seen such a scurrilous bunch.'

Dawlish started down the stairs, but halfway to the bottom he stopped.

'Furtive and scurrilous. If the impression was as obvious as that then it looks to me as if it was the one they intended you to have. Ted, they meant to give you that impression. They knew you were with me, and they've drawn a pretty net about us. Question: shall we let 'em draw it tighter?'

Beresford, just behind him on the stairs, looked startled, and for a moment there was no response. When one did come it was not from Beresford but from a man speaking from above their heads. It was a soft, gentle yet mocking voice, that of a man thoroughly satisfied with himself.

'It has already been drawn tighter,' he said.

Dawlish kept quite still; Beresford looked towards the top of the stairs. He saw no one, and Dawlish saw no one at the foot. He put his hand towards his holster, but before he unfastened the flap the voice came again with an almost sorrowful note.

'You won't resort to violence, now Dawlish, you have too much good sense. We have reached one bargain, we may be able to come to terms on another, but not until you put that gun aside and forget all thought of assault. To be frank, you have added a spice to this affair which I have enjoyed. You have initiative, and that I admire. Go down to the foot of the stairs, and wait there until a door opens.'

It had been uncanny before: it was much worse now. The voice coming from an unseen man, the murkiness of the stairs, the quiet which reigned when no one was speaking, the fact that Dawlish had realised the meaning of the set-up at the Riall Hotel too late, all combined to add to the eeriness of the atmosphere. But none of those things were as important a factor as the calm, confident, faintly mocking note of the unseen speaker's voice.

Beresford said harshly: 'Well, Pat?'

'We'll go down,' said Dawlish, and began to move again. Beresford followed him. When they reached the foot of the stairs they found themselves in a square passage, with three doors leading from it.

They looked at each in turn, but none of them opened.

They heard no sound, the voice remained silent. Dawlish looked over his shoulder towards the top of the stairs, but nothing moved. He realised that the whole theatrical effect was planned to get on their nerves and rattle them, yet even knowing this he could not deny that the ruse was partly successful, for his heart began to thump against his ribs.

He put his hand to his gun again.

'I warned you,' said the voice. Its impact came so suddenly and unexpectedly that they jumped in unison.

Slowly, weirdly, the door immediately ahead of them began to open; they saw into a well-lighted room, but no one appeared on the threshold.

Chapter 16

Friends of Fanessa

Neither Dawlish nor Beresford moved for a moment; then Dawlish glanced sideways at his companion and gave a twisted smile.

'Enter my parlour,' he said, and stepped forward. A little more reluctantly Beresford followed his example.

The room in which they found themselves was long and wide, but with so low a ceiling that Dawlish's head cleared it only by an inch or two. It might have been the lounge of an ultra-modern hotel; the tubular steel furniture was there, and a well-stocked cocktail bar. The usual, fitted carpet covered the floor.

Dawlish turned to see that the door had closed behind them as noiselessly as it had opened. He stepped towards it and tried the handle, but found that it was locked.

Only then was he aware of a distant sound, something which had been there all the time but had made a background and not appeared to affect the silence. It was a thumping noise, and he likened it to the sound of bombs dropping, or gunfire a long way off. It was regular and deliberate.

'What the blazes will happen next?' asked Beresford uneasily. 'I don't know that I like it, Pat.'

'No,' said Dawlish, 'it certainly has disadvantages. I wish – '

He stopped abruptly, for a door behind the cocktail bar opened, and a man in a spotless dinner-jacket stepped through, carrying a small tray on which were four heaps of daintily-cut sandwiches. He put them on the bar, bowed, turned, and disappeared. Dawlish was so surprised that he hardly noticed the man's face.

'Well, well!' exclaimed Beresford.

Dawlish stretched out a ready hand.

'Only hope the damned things aren't poisoned.' He picked

up a sandwich and regarded it with some suspicion, then took an explorative bite. 'Mmm, anchovy. Not bad.'

'You do me less than justice,' the voice assured him. 'They are quite wholesome, Dawlish.'

'I'm reassured,' said Dawlish.

The voice seemed nearer; and the door behind the bar opened again, this time to allow the owner of the voice to enter. Dawlish and Beresford looked at him with some astonishment for the man was extraordinarily good-looking. Middle-aged, suave, superlatively dressed he, in turn, regarded them. A hint of disdain in expression and manner was apparent.

'Good evening,' said Dawlish brightly.

'You are certainly a self-possessed young man, I must admit that,' said the other. 'I expected to find you a little more vociferous in defeat.'

'Defeat?' Dawlish's eyebrows rose. 'What's that?'

'You are experiencing it now,' said the handsome stranger.

'I'm experiencing a new experience,' said Dawlish sunnily. 'After all, reconnoitring behind the enemy lines is one of the essentials of good campaigning, isn't it? By the way, you do know my friend Captain Beresford, don't you?'

The stranger glanced at Beresford and bowed.

'I don't, but my colleagues do,' he said. 'This is all very amusing, Dawlish, but time is running short. I have to finish my work here quickly. Just in case you have some peculiar notions of my inability to plan and prepare, let me tell you that when I heard of Fanessa's unfortunate experience I decided to instruct my London office to allow the girl to go free, believing that you would do the same for Fanessa, and follow him here. You are, of course, of considerable more value as a hostage than Miss Shortt.'

'Is that so?' murmured Dawlish.

'I like to think you are,' said the other suavely. 'However, I must get to the point. How much of this affair do you know?'

'Everything,' Dawlish declared mildly.

'I think that is an exaggeration,' said the other with a sharper note in his voice. 'It would be most unfortunate for you if it were true, Major Dawlish, because – '

'Hush,' said Dawlish. 'In a moment you're going to threaten me. So boring. Threats went out of fashion long ago. They waste time, they give warning, they invite, for the swollen-headed jackasses who utter them, the fall which so swiftly follows. Do I make myself clear?'

The other eyed Dawlish thoughtfully.

'Even in the face of such eloquence I must insist that it would not be safe for anyone to know *all* about this affair.'

'No?' mused Dawlish. 'Still, safe or not, I do assure you that what I haven't been told I've put together.' He bit into another sandwich. 'Scrambled egg,' he added brightly, 'and they've actually remembered the salt.'

'I don't want to lose patience with you, Dawlish.'

'Of course you don't,' said Dawlish warmly. 'You're the most patient of men, I can tell that at once. Let me see now; the position is this. I am in an underground room, I can be seen by someone outside these walls, there may or may not be several guns trained on me. You are about to make me an offer, and if I accept it I can go free, but if I don't you will arrange to kill me. I wonder if I've overlooked anything?' he added, and frowned questioningly at Beresford. 'What do you think, Ted?'

Beresford pursed his lips.

'Very aptly put, old chap. Couldn't do better myself.'

There was a long pause.

'Ah! I knew I'd overlooked something!' said Dawlish, and with the air of a man to whom everything was suddenly clear. 'The difference between you and other people is that you *really mean all you say.* That's it, isn't it? Won't you have a sandwich?'

With a sudden, savage movement the stranger snatched the tray of sandwiches and flung it into Dawlish's face. The action was so instinctive, so unexpected, that there was no time to dodge. The sandwiches struck the large man, and fell forlornly to the floor.

'Well, well,' murmured Dawlish. 'What a waste!'

'Listen to me,' said the other, his voice no longer suave but harsh with anger. 'Unless you stop talking nonsense I shall give you no opportunity to leave here. I have a proposition to put to you. Do you wish to hear it?'

Dawlish said, lightly: 'Certainly. But do step warily, trodden-in egg can make such an awful mess.'

The other swallowed convulsively.

'You are aware, I take it, that I have the custody of Dr Shortt. I shall afford him every facility for his experiments, and if he has the sense to realise it he will be much better off with me. But – I need Brunning as well. Shortt without Brunning is useless to me, and Brunning without Shortt is useless to anyone. Posslethwaite is obstinate, he believes that he can keep Brunning safe. He is quite wrong, Dawlish. I shall wait for another twenty-four hours, and then I shall kill Shortt. Posslethwaite will not want that any more than I do, but I have – '

'Come to the end of your patience?' suggested Dawlish politely.

'I have warned you enough already,' said the man in front of him with a tone of such harshness in his voice that it surprised even Dawlish: it bespoke an anger which made the man shake in the grip of a passion which, although held in check, was very much like Jones's. 'Can you persuade Brunning to come here? Or Posslethwaite to release him? Your only chance of personal freedom is to do that.'

The name 'Brunning' was entirely fresh to Dawlish. It was a link for which he had sounded Posslethwaite in vain. Secretly elated he appeared to ponder.

'Well, can you?' snapped the other.

'I suppose I could try,' began Dawlish.

'Trying is of no use. Either you can or you can't.'

'In that case – ' began Dawlish.

'Give me a plain yes or no, damn you!'

Dawlish said slowly: 'That is impossible. I – '

He stopped abruptly.

The man in front of him raised his hand. There was a moment of complete silence, and then a whirring sound: part of the blank wall on one side of the room opened to reveal a white screen, like that of a small private cinema.

Figures moved across it, men, women, houses.

It was sudden and startling enough to be unnerving, and Dawlish heard Beresford mutter under his breath. Dawlish realised that he had seen such films before, uncensored as were these; it was a typical German horror film. And suddenly the room was filled with the droning of bombers; like little specks they appeared on a corner of the screen and drew ominously nearer. From the picture, too, there came the wail of the sirens as the people moved like mad things, hither and thither. The bombers drew nearer, and then the bombs began to fall, and there was horror beyond words. The room was filled with the shrieking and the crying and the noise of sudden death.

The scene suddenly switched to a tiny village. Peasants were shown, working in the fields.

Then came the tanks.

All the miscellany of Nazi horror was portrayed in the screen, even to the raping and the hanging, the burning and the torture of men and women and children. Dawlish had seen many such exhibitions because he had reported upon them; but he had seen none so bestial as this. There was no limit to the sadist-mind which conceived the happenings and the picture.

And then there came to the screen a single man, standing against a wall, with his arms raised above his head and his wrists fastened by cords to nails. And then men with knives and others with burning brands of fire approached him. For what seemed a long time he kept silent, his lips tightening, his neck swelling, the veins at his forehead coming up and sweat rolling down his cheeks.

Then he began to groan –

Soon the room was filled only with the sound of his cries, but as they faded, although they continued in the background, gutteral voices sounded afresh, all of them asking questions. Shadows appeared on the wall, shadows of men in the stiff peaked hats of the Gestapo. The questions increased in number, grew more insistent, the tortured body by the wall sagged, the eyes opened, words spilled from his mouth.

The film ceased abruptly, and there was deep silence in the room.

The handsome man, who seemed so courteous when he had first entered, began to speak in a voice soft and low-pitched and seeming to come from a long way off.

'We can do that to you, Dawlish,' he said. 'And to Beresford. I wish to know whether you can and will bring Brunning to me. I will allow you to go, but keep Beresford here. You will guess what will happen to Beresford if you fail in your mission. Now will you answer me yes or no – now that you know what the consequences of failure will be?'

Chapter 17

Dawlish Gives His Answer

Dawlish heard the voice but did not see the man: he was seeing the pictures which had been on the screen, and hearing the cacophony of noise which had accompanied it. He felt a cold rage which made him bunch his hands by his sides, and he set his teeth and compressed his lips, not trusting himself to speak.

He had believed that this affair might be connected with espionage; now he knew that it was.

The grey-haired man said: 'Well, Dawlish?'

And again:

'*Well*, Dawlish?'

Dawlish said slowly: 'If I try to get Brunning, I don't do it on my own.'

'Exactly what do you mean?' the other demanded.

'I do it with Beresford,' Dawlish said.

'I have told you my conditions!' snapped the grey-haired man, and his eyes showed the anger which had been in them when he had first given the signal for the films to be shown.

'And I've told you mine,' said Dawlish.

'Dawlish, there are eight men here. They are engaged at the moment, but I can postpone their other work and bring them into this room. Many things have happened in this room. If the carpet is rolled up you will see the signs of many interviews with men who thought they had the courage to withstand my persuasion.'

Dawlish held his hand in front of him, large, well-formed, with flat-topped fingers and a lined palm. It shook like that of a man with palsy. Beresford uttered a sharp exclamation, but Dawlish did not look at his friend.

The man with the handsome face stared at the shaking hand, then, smiling, took a step forward: and then Dawlish moved, swiftly, sharply, gripping the other's wrist, so that the man spun round, gasping in sudden pain: and in a moment Dawlish had him with his back against him, his right arm twisted upwards in a half-Nelson. It all happened so swiftly that Beresford began and finished an exclamation throughout its course. Dawlish held the man still, and said nothing. There was no sound but his victim's harsh breathing.

Then slowly:

'Not so good,' said Dawlish in a clear voice. 'If your little friends use their guns they'll get you first, my poppet, and if they try to make a rear approach I'll break your arm and start on the other. *Tell them to come in here.*'

The man so helplessly in his grip muttered:

'I – I don't know that they'll obey.'

'They will if you tell them to,' said Dawlish confidently. He pulled the man backwards with him, rounded the bar, and reached the door through which the waiter had come with sandwiches. 'Stand by the other door, Ted. You can use your gun if they try anything and I'll finish off this devil's disciple. But I don't think they'd like him killed.'

Beresford nodded, and stepped briskly towards the door.

Both of them knew, as he took his revolver from its holster, that it might be the signal for a burst of shooting from the walls or the ceiling; there was no guarantee that the hold which Dawlish had over the grey-haired man would be sufficient protection. But it appeared to be, for nothing happened. Beresford took up a position by the door, gun in hand, and Dawlish eased his own revolver from its holster, maintaining his grip on his victim's arm.

'Send for them,' he ordered sharply.

There was a moment's pause; and then the man raised his voice. There was a note of fear, almost of hysteria in it.

'You won't get away with this, you can't get away!'

'Send for them,' repeated Dawlish, and gave the slightest of increased pressure to his grip on the man's arm. He heard the man gasp, and then call out:

'All – all of you. Come in.'

Dawlish said nothing else, believing that those who could see what was happening would have the sense to understand that if they tried trickery it would mean the death of their leader. After a short pause the door in the far corner opened and two men appeared.

One of them carried an automatic, and Beresford stretched out his hand. Absurdly into the dead silence of the room, came his single simple exhortation.

'Gimme,' said Beresford.

The man looked at him; he was a blunt-faced fellow with short grey hair. He licked his lips, his small eyes darted furtively to and fro; and then he released his hold on the gun. He just dropped it. Dawlish imagined that he hoped Beresford would stoop to pick it up and perhaps render himself open to attack. Dawlish smiled serenly, for Beresford said:

'Now pick it up!'

Again there was a pause, and then, very slowly, the man obeyed.

The second man, also armed, did the same. Beresford let the door close, and then told them to turn their backs towards him. They obeyed, and one by one he ran over their clothes to make sure that any concealed weapons were brought into the open. From each man he obtained a small automatic, and dropped them into his capacious pocket, making no comment at all.

All the time the man in Dawlish's grip stared at them furiously. Dawlish could almost sympathise with him. He did not move, however, but said cheerfully:

'Have a look outside, Ted, there might be others. If you're not back in five minutes I'll finish off this little squirt and worry about it afterwards.'

'I'll be back,' said Beresford with confidence.

A warm glow of relief and satisfaction took possession of Dawlish. He did not relax his grip, but waited, watching the two men by the other wall. For the moment he held the upper hand. But there might be limits to his immunity; it might not be possible for him to get out of the Riall Hotel while taking the other as protection. But for the moment there was no need to worry.

Beresford returned inside the five minutes which Dawlish had stipulated.

'There's another room on the other side of this, Pat. But no one's there, though there's some noise going on downstairs.'

'Downstairs?' Dawlish was surprised.

'Yes, there's another flight of stairs. Have you heard the bumping?' Dawlish nodded, and Beresford went on: 'It seems to have stopped now. I fancy there was a third man with these hoboes, who hurried downstairs to tell the main party of the trouble.'

Dawlish waited for more.

'There's a steel door across the head of the stairs,' said Beresford, obviously very pleased, 'and it works by pressing a switch. I couldn't find a switch on the inside, so I pressed the outside one and the party below are cut off for the time being. Fair going?' he added hopefully.

Dawlish smiled.

'Fair enough. Is there a control switch on the other side of that door?' he added, leaning forward and speaking more closely to the ear of his captive.

The man said nothing.

'Is there?' repeated Dawlish, exerting a little extra pressure.

'Stop that!' the man gasped. 'You'll break my arm! No, no, no! It's a one-way switch, it can only be operated from the outside!'

'I hope that's the truth,' said Dawlish, and released the man. But before the other staggered forward Dawlish slipped a hand inside the man's inner pocket, and drew out a wallet.

In it were two letters, each addressed to:

Charles Lavington, Esq.,
Riall Hotel, Cross Street,
Manchester.

There were several cards and a cheque book, all of which bore the same name. Dawlish nodded thoughtfully.

'I wonder what your real name is? I suppose Lavington will do for the time being.' He paused. 'What's happening downstairs?'

Lavington muttered: 'You'll learn in time.'

Dawlish repeated quietly: 'What's happening downstairs?' He pulled Lavington round to face him.

The man's eyes were bloodshot, his face was streaked with perspiration, he seemed to have aged years in the past twenty minutes. As if compelled by the glitter in Dawlish's eyes, he said harshly:

'Breaking into – the cellar – next door.'

'I see,' said Dawlish. 'The Riall Safe Deposit. How many men are there?'

'Five or six,' muttered Lavington.

'Not too much of a handful,' said Dawlish. 'Ted, I think Tim might be back by now. He'll be waiting about outside. Get him down, will you? If anyone should be about, deal with 'em.' He smiled a little vaguely. 'And on the way back, better close the street door. We don't want the police inquiring at this stage.'

When Beresford had gone out the room was very quiet. Dawlish no longer looked through the papers and the wallet, but put them all into his pocket, and regarded Lavington.

He felt reasonably secure.

He believed that the other had been so sure of himself that he had taken no further precautions, and provided the steel door was accessible only from the outside, there was no other danger from the hotel. The situation was not so simple as it might seem, however. He now knew the name 'Brunning', but he wanted other information, and believed that by exerting the requisite pressure he could obtain it.

So he said: 'Why are you so anxious to get Brunning, Lavington?'

The man said, spitefully: 'I thought you knew everything!'

'Not motives,' said Dawlish. 'Only facts.' When there was no answer, he mused: 'Do you want Brunning here or in Germany, I wonder?'

There was only the slightest change of expression on Lavington's face, but it was enough to make Dawlish sure that he had scored a point. He had known from the moment the horror picture had been flashed on to the screen that his earlier suspicions were justified and this was a matter of espionage. Beyond that, and the fact that the Nazis wanted Brunning very badly indeed, there was nothing he could safely guess. It would be unwise to take too many chances. As it was he was aware of furtive glances from the captive men, could almost hear their minds working as they tried to evolve a way of attack which would deal with Dawlish and at the same time do nothing to injure Lavington.

The door opened and Ted came in with Tim Jeremy on his heels.

'Now we can get moving,' said Dawlish briskly. 'We want to put these folk out of action for the time being. I don't think we could trust 'em not to run away.'

Beresford said: 'I saw a coil of rope outside.'

'Good fellow. We'll commandeer it.'

It took less than five minutes for the three of them to make reasonably sure that none of their captives could get free or raise an alarm. They worked with speed and competence, and not without reason were thoroughly pleased with themselves. Dawlish even hummed a tune beneath his breath, but when the task was done he straightened up seriously enough.

'The target for tonight is downstairs,' he said briefly.

As they left the room, Beresford told Dawlish that the street door was now locked, and the man behind the settee, though conscious, was also helpless.

'And no signs of anyone else?'

'None at all.'

'I fancy that they keep the place for their own brood,' said Dawlish. 'Not a bad idea, when you work it out. Now, where is this steel door?'

Beresford led the way through a narrow passage, and they entered another room; from it Dawlish could see into the room which they had just left. He was tempted to suggest that Tim should stay there to make sure no one else appeared, but he decided against it.

The problem now was that of the five men below.

They were, of course, trying to get through to the safe deposit; not only had Lavington said so, but it was the obvious thing to do. The safe deposit, and the fact that Posslethwaite had talked of it and given him, Dawlish, a key to a private box, was likely to yield information of considerable value.

The steel door was across one corner of a small, square room, which was quite empty of things or people. Dawlish pressed the electric switch down, Beresford close against one wall, he and Tim pressed against the other. The door began to slide open.

Dawlish hardly knew what to expect.

A fusilade of gunfire would not have surprised him; nor would a man advancing in obvious fear and carrying something to serve as a white flag. Either of these things were possible.

He thought, too, that the party trapped below stairs might try to rush the doorway in a bunch, firing as they came, for he felt quite certain that whoever had carried the bad tidings to them had made it clear that they were in desperate straits.

He waited for perhaps ten seconds, with bated breath.

Then Tim Jeremy gasped, and Dawlish stared, as nearly

110

stupefied as events were ever likely to make him. For from the other side of the door strode a stalwart policeman in uniform, flashing a torch, wearing a steel helmet, and with a truncheon held determinedly in front of him.

Chapter 18

The Police Are Inquisitive

Dawlish was too surprised even to exclaim.

The policeman saw him, took a firmer grip on his truncheon, and advanced still further, heedless of or indifferent to the guns which each man held. Dawlish recognised him; it was the man who had passed him outside the Safe Deposit and whom he had thought to be in some degree suspicious.

Instead of speaking to them, the policeman raised his voice, obviously for the benefit of someone beneath him.

'All right, sir, I've got 'em!'

It was perfect, thought Dawlish: the poise, the confidence, the utter refusal to believe that he could come to any harm. There was just a possibility that the man was a fraud, that the uniform had been donned by one of Lavington's men in order to make a getaway; and yet he could not believe that, and when he saw two more men come up, burly fellows as obviously Lancashire natives as Fanessa, for instance, was Italian, any lingering fears he had were dissipated.

The 'sir' of the policeman's summons was a tall, sharp-faced individual in plainclothes, who came in briskly, and spoke directly to Dawlish.

'If you try to use those guns you'll only make it worse for yourself. Come quietly, and it'll be easier.'

Policemen streamed into the room, crowding it, shouldering the three men in army uniform, making their guns useless even had they been inclined to try to use them. Only when they were going towards the other door, and the passage, did Dawlish say:

'Officer – have a look at this, will you?'

He had a card in his hand – the one which authorised him to do many unlikely things, and which he knew would make this man alter his attitude. At first the fellow was suspicious and even contemptuous, but the signature on the card caught his eye, and he frowned.

'What's that?... Major Dawlish – ' He looked sharply into Dawlish's face. 'I've heard of you before today – here, were you at Mere Street?'

Dawlish's mind was working at high speed. Lavington was in the other room and, unless Dawlish found some way of making sure that police suspicions of the man were dispelled, would be taken away with his accomplices. Dawlish cared nothing for the others, but he wanted Lavington free for the time being, or rather, at his disposal, not that of the police. He said quickly:

'I thought we had a lead on you, but you're smarter up here than I expected! Did you get the crowd downstairs?'

'We did,' said the plainclothes man.

'Had they broken through into the Safe Deposit?' asked Dawlish quickly.

'They had – and we thought you were after the same thing,' said the other. 'They said there were three more men up here, and – ' He smiled a little grimly. 'I expect there will be time for explanations later, sir. You'll understand me if I say that I must search the place quickly, won't you?'

That, thought Dawlish, was tantamount to saying that he was not fully satisfied with the authenticity of the card, and that he did not propose to allow Dawlish to act for him. The challenge was unspoken, but nevertheless there, and Dawlish admired the other for it. He smiled, and rubbed the bridge of his nose thoughtfully, seeing only one hope.

'Three, are there? Oh, yes – there's the receptionist upstairs. Quite a band of buddies. One bunch after the Safe Deposit, the other on a kidnapping errand.'

'Kidnapping?' The detective's voice rose a shade.

'No less,' said Dawlish without batting an eye. 'They've taken possession of a man named Lavington, who's my particular meat. He's in the other room,' added Dawlish. 'I heard that there were more of them getting through to the Deposit, and thought I ought to try to do something about it. May I know your name?'

'Mickle,' said the detective promptly. 'Detective Sergeant Mickle of the Manchester C.I.D.' He took out a card, handed it to Dawlish, and then said briskly: 'Is your Mr Lavington safe?'

'I think so,' said Dawlish. 'He was bound hand and foot when we arrived, and I hadn't time to unfasten him, so I

113

served the others with the same treatment and left them all together.

'Indeed,' said Mickle.

Dawlish wondered if he were deceived. It would be awkward if he were not, for a check with Whitehall might undo all that was so far done. For Dawlish could only see Lavington as the means of finding the real truth behind the affair of Dr Shortt.

And then he was visited by inspiration.

When he had led the police into the other room, and the trio on the floor were untied, he went close enough to Lavington to mutter:

'Keep your mouth shut, we're supposed to be friends.'

Lavington showed no sign that he understood, but Dawlish believed that he had heard, and would have the sense to act on it.

Dawlish turned to Mickle.

'How much longer are we going to be here?'

'I don't know,' said Mickle. 'Why?'

'I ought to 'phone Whitehall,' said Dawlish.

'There's no reason why you shouldn't do it from here, is there?' asked Mickle, and Dawlish supposed that there was not.

He was accompanied by a youthful policeman to the upstairs lounge, and used the telephone in the reception bureau. The constable stood near enough to hear what he said, and was obviously under instructions to do so from Mickle. Dawlish put the call through to Colonel Whitehead's Whitehall office, but was not surprised when a girl told him that Whitehead had left.

'Put me through to his house, please,' Dawlish said. In a few moments he heard the mellow voice of Colonel Whitehead, who had no idea at all that Dawlish was doing anything more than resting at Clay House.

'Yes, Dawlish,' said Whitehead, in the tone of a man who had little time to spare. To Dawlish's ears there came a fragment of music, and he knew at once that Whitehead was staging one of his many official parties.

Without looking at the constable Dawlish said with deep and evident satisfaction:

'I've got Lavington, sir. I thought you should know.'

There was a pause.

It surprised Dawlish, for he expected Whitehead to de-

114

mand with some acerbity why he had Lavington; who was Lavington; and why he considered it necessary to drag him, Whitehead, from his beloved music to be told that Lavington was caught. There was no such outburst, only the silence, which grew prolonged.

'Are you still there?' Dawlish asked at last.

'Yes,' said Whitehead, in the low-pitched voice of a man recovering from a surprise of major proportions. 'So you've got Lavington! As long as I live I'll never understand you, Dawlish, I'll never know what's in that mind of yours. Why, damn your eyes!' roared Whitehead. 'I didn't know that you were after him! I didn't even know that you'd heard of him!' He drew another deep breath, while Dawlish gulped, glanced again at the constable, and tried to understand what this was all about. Whitehead knew of Lavington, that was the incredible thing. Whitehead was not surprised by the name.

'I hadn't heard of him as Lavington until a few days ago,' went on Whitehead in that strained, incredulous voice. 'I hadn't the heart to put you on to him, I thought you needed a weekend's rest. And you come calmly to the telephone and tell me you've got him! Are you sure?' asked Whitehead more sharply. 'You haven't made a mistake?'

'Oh, this is Lavington,' said Dawlish, breaking out into a gentle sweat. 'Charles Lavington. Aged about fifty, handsome as they make 'em, something of a dandy –'

'Yes, that's him. Where are you?'

'In Manchester.'

'Manchester! What on earth –' Whitehead broke off again, uttered another word which Dawlish did not catch, and then began to laugh.

Dawlish smiled dutifully, looking a little sheepish. There were many things he did not understand, but this completely took his breath away.

Whitehead recovered at last, and said with more decorum: 'I'll let you share the joke later, Dawlish. Meanwhile hold on to Lavington as if he were made of Dresden china, don't let him go, and don't – he's not hurt, is he?'

'Not seriously,' said Dawlish.

'Good. We want a lot from that fine gentleman, and we need it in a hurry. My oath, Dawlish, I've had some surprises but nothing to beat that, even from you. I shall want to know what the devil you mean by going off on your own like that and getting into the case, too! Still, that's neither here nor there.'

'No,' said Dawlish in a strangled voice. 'The thing is, the Manchester police might want to interview him. I thought you would prefer – '

'Don't you let the police have anything to do with him,' said Whitehead sharply. 'Look after him yourself.'

'Will you telephone the necessary authority?' asked Dawlish. 'I don't know that I've convinced them yet.'

'Leave that to me,' said Whitehead. 'You bring Lavington to London. The quicker the better, and I think you'd best come by road. Hm, yes. I'll get something arranged. Where can I find you, for the time being?'

'I'll stay here, I think,' said Dawlish. After glancing at the number disc on the instrument, he repeated it. Whitehead repeated it in turn, and then rang off.

Dawlish passed a hand over his damp forehead, and smiled upon the constable. He was not surprised to find that Mickle was dubious about staying at the Riall Hotel. However, he agreed that it could be done. The two low-brows were brought upstairs, handcuffed to policemen, and after them the other men from the cellar next to the Safe Deposit.

One thing surprised Dawlish: Fanessa was not of their number. He said nothing, however, and smiled amiably at Lavington as that worthy, his poise returned, came up in the rear of the prisoners. Not one of his men had given him away, and he smiled upon Dawlish as on an old friend.

'I owe you a great deal, a great deal,' he said ironically. 'Believe me, I shall not forget it.'

'I'm sure you won't,' murmured Dawlish.

'And now, officer,' said Lavington to Mickle, 'I have an important meeting to attend, and I hope – '

'Oh, don't worry about that,' said Dawlish airily. 'It's been cancelled. I've just been informed. I'll look after you.'

Lavington gave him one sharp, expressive glance, quickly shrouded.

'That's very good of you indeed,' he said warmly.

Mickle busied himself on the telephone. The prisoners were taken away. One constable and Mickle remained in the lounge, others were busy searching the downstairs rooms. Mickle, still a little restrained, thawed enough to tell Dawlish that the constable on patrol duty had thought he had seen something suspicious at the Safe Deposit, and gone down to investigate.

Dawlish beamed.

'It couldn't have been simpler, could it? I wonder what they were after?'

Mickle shrugged his shoulders meaningly.

'An hour inside, and they would have escaped with a tidy sum, Major Dawlish. Half the jewels of Manchester are kept there.'

The telephone rang.

Mickle answered it. He spoke with obvious respect, listened for perhaps two minutes, then, after a final 'yes, sir', turned to face Dawlish. The change in his attitude was almost ludicrous. Dawlish's *bona fides* were in perfect order, and all suspicion of him was now withdrawn.

'Apparently you've only told me half a story,' said Mickle with some appreciation. 'It must be pretty big, Major, or Sir Harold wouldn't have attended to it himself. There will be a police car at your disposal in half-an-hour's time, and an escort car with it. That's what you're expecting, I think?'

'More or less,' said Dawlish, silently congratulating Whitehead on his speed. 'Many thanks.'

'I'm glad to have been able to help,' said Mickle. 'Is there anything else I can do for you?'

Dawlish smiled tentatively.

'Well, you've been very good. There are just a few telephone calls I would like to make, of an essentially secret nature.'

Mickle nodded understandingly and withdrew.

The door closed.

The restraint which had fallen upon Beresford and Jeremy fell away. They were sitting on either side of the settee, with Lavington between them.

'Pat, what – '

'Easy does it,' cautioned Dawlish. 'There'll be plenty of time for explanations later, but we've caught a big fish. Haven't we, Lavington? A bigger fish than we knew of, and we're fully authorised to deal with him as we feel inclined. Watch him.' He pulled the telephone towards him.

In a few seconds he was connected with Posslethwaite, at King's Road.

It had been apparent for some time that he would not be able to make a return trip to the nursing home that night,

117

and he wanted to give Posslethwaite some idea of what was happening without being too informative.

'Ah've been expecting you to ring through,' Posslethwaite said promptly. 'Have you lost him?'

'Him?' echoed Dawlish. 'Oh, Fanessa. D'you know, I think I have! But wait a moment. Does the name Lavington mean anything to you?'

'Ah can't recall it,' said Posslethwaite after a pause. 'Why, where does he come in?'

'I'm in the process of finding out,' said Dawlish. 'And I'll be going to London to do it. I'll keep the rules as far as I can, but you should know one thing. Espionage is the word.'

'Are you sure?' asked Posslethwaite sharply.

'Quite sure,' said Dawlish.

The other man was silent for an appreciable time, then declared that in view of the wider issues he would have to leave everything in Dawlish's hands. He impressed upon Dawlish the need for keeping Shortt out of prison: his insistence on that was one of the most puzzling features of the case, thought Dawlish, who was only now acclimatising himself to the fact that the whole affair was much, much larger than he had at first imagined.

He rang off, and as he turned, Lavington jumped from the settee.

'D-Dawlish, I don't know what nonsense this is about espionage, but I assure you that I have nothing to do with it, nothing at all. Moreover, you are making a big mistake in trusting Posslethwaite. The man is a bigger rogue than – than — '

'You are?' asked Dawlish amiably.

Lavington licked his lips.

'If you allow yourself to be victimised by Posslethwaite you will live to regret it, he – he is a complete rogue.' Dawlish's eyes creased at the corners and Beresford and Jeremy regarded Lavington with questioning expressions and no great tolerance. 'I am serious,' Lavington went on earnestly. 'Posslethwaite is a dangerous man, he – he – '

'Well?'

'This is damnable!' Lavington continued in a shrill voice. 'Dawlish, I have no idea what you think I am doing, but I can prove that I am not engaged in espionage.' The man spoke so confidently that it was almost possible to believe what he said. 'I – I tried a trick on you downstairs, I was not

118

serious, I should not dream of using such methods as depicted in the film – '

'Or under the carpet?' murmured Dawlish.

'Listen to me!' screamed Lavington. 'I tried to frighten you, that was legitimate enough, I do want Brunning, I have powerful private reasons for that. But don't fool yourself, Dawlish, *don't think Posslethwaite is a friend of Dr Shortt's.* Nor that nauseating creature Jones, they are Shortt's enemies, deadly enemies. If there is espionage in this matter then Posslethwaite is responsible for it. *I* am not.'

'And I suppose Posslethwaite employs Fanessa and your other hoodlums,' said Dawlish mildly.

Lavington licked his lips.

'No, they are in my employ, but Posslethwaite has succeeded in deceiving you, that is obvious. You will be making a fatal error if you allow him to continue doing so. Rather than be in *his* hands, Shortt would remain voluntarily with me. He would have no doubt which was the safer place.'

In spite of himself Dawlish felt the stirring of uncertainty.

'If I am not telling the truth, why has Posslethwaite avoided the police?' demanded Lavington in the same shrill voice. 'Ask yourself that, Dawlish! If it were just that he wanted to get Shortt back for a genuine reason of goodwill why should he evade the police? And why should he persuade Amelia Shortt and Bingham that the police must not be approached?'

Both of the men sitting with Lavington looked up into Dawlish's eyes, and Dawlish knew that they were asking silent questions; the very ones he was asking himself.

He had no faith at all in Lavington's protestation, was fully aware that the man, now cornered and desperate, was trying to put suspicion on Posslethwaite in the hope of making his captors less wary of him. Nevertheless, he had awakened a certain curiosity and uneasiness in Dawlish's mind. Why *had* Posslethwaite been so reluctant to go to the police?

He had declared that he was thinking of Dr Shortt. *Only* of Dr Shortt.

Dawlish began to wonder, disturbed because the poison from Lavington's tongue was having some effect.

Then footsteps sounded on the stairs leading from the street, and there was a tap on the door.

Chapter 19

Mr Lavington Is Spritely

The caller was a policeman, there to tell them that the car was waiting outside. Dawlish said that they would be going down immediately, and then thought regretfully of the sandwiches which Lavington had thrown at him. He knew that there would be little prospect of getting food on the way, and was in fact doubtful whether Whitehead had been wise to arrange for them to travel by road. It would add hours to the journey, and all of them would be tired when they reached London. It was a time, Dawlish thought, when they would need all their wits about them.

He went downstairs for a word with Mickle, who was going through some papers. The cinema had been discovered, a reel of film was on the floor by Mickle's side. He pulled a face as he touched it with his foot.

'Have you seen that?' he asked.

Dawlish nodded.

Mickle leaned forward and lifted a locked brief-case from a chair. On it, in black, were the initials 'R.A.L.', and Dawlish had little doubt that they were Lavington's.

'I haven't tried to open this,' said Mickle. 'It's your friend Mr Lavington's, I imagine.'

'Ah, thanks.' Dawlish tucked the case under his arm, hoping and believing that something of importance was in it. 'You've been a tower of strength, Mickle. I do appreciate it.'

'I've just done my job,' said Mickle with some embarrassment. 'Is there anything else you want?'

'Have you come across any sandwiches?' said Dawlish unexpectedly. 'Apart from those on the floor, I mean.'

'Oh, yes,' said Mickle at once. 'There's a little pile here – I think they were all prepared to leave after they'd finished next door, and these had been made for the journey.' He led the way into a small kitchen where, on a white cloth, were several piles of sandwiches. Gratefully Dawlish packed half of them, and then went upstairs to find Lavington protesting volubly to Beresford:

'I will make the payment in cash, I assure you. You will have every penny, *every* penny.'

Beresford raised an eyebrow towards Dawlish.

'Bribery and corruption, no less. He doesn't appear to believe in the incorruptible man.'

'Well, he's not likely to have met one among his own pals,' said Dawlish.

He led the way briskly to the door. Beresford and Jeremy followed, Lavington between them. Tim held his right arm, Ted his left. They reached the door, and in order to get through Beresford had to release the man and step behind him.

Lavington chose that moment to act.

He kicked sideways at Jeremy, wrenched himself away, then ducked to one side, avoiding a quick grab from Beresford.

Dawlish, warned by a gasp from Jeremy, half-turned; then Lavington hurled himself bodily at him. Dawlish grabbed at the single handrail, gripped it, but lost his balance. Lavington struck savagely, scrambling over Dawlish's outstretched legs.

They were only a few steps down, there were a dozen or more steps ahead of them.

Dawlish, releasing his grip on the hand-rail, slithered downward. Flinging out an arm, he managed to catch Lavington's ankle. The hold was slight, but it was enough to bring the man crashing to the ground.

Slowly, Dawlish picked himself up.

'Well, well,' he said a little bemusedly. 'Caught napping, were we?'

He did not need to do anything more himself, for Beresford and Jeremy hurried past him. Between them they picked Lavington up. He was dazed, and his forehead was bleeding a little, but his eyes were open.

'You won't be so spritely for a while,' said Beresford unkindly.

As he spoke the door of the hotel opened, and a man in police uniform asked if there was anything the matter. Dawlish assured him that there was nothing of consequence. He moved, a little stiffly, to a large car drawn up outside

the front door. A smaller one stood just behind it. A uniformed policeman approached him.

'Major Dawlish?'

'That's right,' said Dawlish.

'I can put a chauffeur at your disposal, sir, or you can
drive yourself. Yours is the large car. The smaller one will
follow as far as Hatton to make sure that you're all right.'

'Hatton?' asked Dawlish.

'The airfield, sir,' said the policeman.

'An airfield, is it?' asked Dawlish, and was immediately
suspicious, for Whitehead had said nothing about flying.

Nevertheless it was a more cheerful prospect than going
by road, but before he took the policeman's word he sent
Tim Jeremy for Mickle. The detective-sergeant identified the
uniformed police, and, in a happier frame of mind, Dawlish
decided that as the police knew the road better than he did,
it would be wiser to let them drive. Lavington, still bemused
from the crack on the head, was half-lifted into the back of
the big car, and they started off.

The driver was not talkative, but answered promptly
enough when Dawlish spoke.

'Hatton isn't the usual airfield for Manchester, is it?'

'No, sir, Hatton's a military 'drome. We had instructions
that a 'plane would be waiting there to take you to London.'

'Who from?' asked Dawlish.

'Sir Harold Kilby.'

At the back of Dawlish's mind there was an uncomfortable feeling that all was not well. He wished that Whitehead
had spoken of going by air, although he told himself that he
had probably changed his mind at the last moment and
decided that it was not worth advising Dawlish of so elementary change in the means of transit. Nevertheless the
uneasiness remained with Dawlish as they drove through
the built-up area of the town. He had no idea in which direction they were going. Soon he missed the dark, squat build-
ings on either side of him, saw telegraph poles stretching
upwards against the starlit sky. Now and again they passed
a solitary car, and once a small convoy of lorries came towards them, the lights from the vehicles forcing the driver
to slow down.

After half-an-hour, Dawlish asked: 'How much further?'

'About another ten minutes, sir,' he was told.

The driver was certain of himself, giving no suggestion at

all that Dawlish's fears were justified; and yet they remained. The escort car followed, keeping about fifty yards behind them. Everything seemed all right, and yet the quiet was uncanny.

Dawlish began to toy with the idea that Mickle might not be all that he seemed.

Then he caught a glimpse of the red light of a stationary car. At the head of it was a man waving a torch. The driver of Dawlish's car pulled up; a man in police uniform approached them.

Dawlish saw that half-a-dozen vehicles, mostly lorries, were pulled up ahead of them; it was a traffic block of some kind, the last thing to be expected on a lonely stretch of country road. Very much on the alert, he spoke as the driver wound the driving-window down.

'What's the trouble here?'

'I'd like to see your identification cards, please. Special orders just come through,' said the man outside. 'There's been a spot of trouble at the aerodrome.'

He held a hand through the window as the driver took out his wallet, and Dawlish did the same. Yet even while it was happening Dawlish's fears increased; there was something wrong about this as there had been about the whole journey.

Then, quite suddenly, he saw the flaw.

The man had asked for 'identification' cards. He should have asked for registration cards, although the mistake was a common enough one to the general public. *The general public*, thought Dawlish, not to a policeman.

He said quietly: 'Trouble ahead, Tim.' He put his wallet back and put a hand to his holster, and at the same time opened his door. But even as he did so figures approached from the side of the road, three or four men, and one of them had a gun. He made that obvious because he fired, and the bullet whistled over Dawlish's head and the roof of the car.

A voice rasped: 'Stay just where you are.'

'Well, well,' thought Dawlish. 'If it isn't our old friend Fanessa again.'

He saw the tall figure of the erstwhile prisoner shining a torch into the rear of the cab, where Lavington was pushing Beresford and Jeremy aside. The two large men were helpless; from the opposite window a man was covering them with a revolver.

Dawlish felt his arms gripped, and a hand snatched at his holster. The hold-up was complete and thorough. Lavington jumped from the car, as spritely as ever he had been.

'My case!' he snapped. 'Dawlish has my case!'

So he'd noticed that, thought Dawlish.

It was very dark except for the beam of light concentrated on the interior of the big car. Dawlish saw Fanessa alter the direction of the torch as he moved forward to look for the brief-case. Dawlish dropped downwards, then shot a hand through the open door of the car, and gripping the sleeve of Fanessa's coat, pulled him off balance.

At the same time he roared: 'Help, there! *Help!*'

A bullet whined over his head. He caught a glimpse of Lavington in the light of Fanessa's torch as it fell to the ground. The man had obtained a gun, and was glaring at him wild-eyed.

It was in that moment that Dawlish gave up all reasonable hope of preventing Lavington from escaping, knew that he would be lucky to get out of this with his life. It was a brief, tense period unpleasant as any he had ever experienced. He scrambled from the car, hitting the ground heavily, saw the flash of another shot – and then heard footsteps.

Only then did he realise that his cries for help had been answered, that the drivers from the lorries and cars held up ahead of him were rushing towards the spot.

Quickly, craftily, Lavington slipped away.

Dawlish, setting thought of everything else aside, managed to get to his feet and plunged after the other man, who disappeared from view. In the sudden glare of a headlight Dawlish picked him up again, crouching near the hedge with two of his men. Dawlish felt for his gun, and discovered that it was missing. Taking a desperate chance, he leapt towards the hedge while Lavington, hoisted by the two men, was halfway over it.

Dawlish grabbed at his foot.

Lavington came tumbling down on top of him, but then the two men launched themselves at Dawlish, and he was powerless to fend them off. Someone kicked him viciously in the ribs. He felt a heavy weight descend on the back of his neck, followed by a sharp pain; then he lost consciousness.

*

124

Ted Beresford, one large hand gripping Lavington's forearm, stared anxiously down at the unconscious figure of his friend. A policeman, kneeling by Dawlish's side, nodded reassuringly.

Beresford's terror subsided.

The lorry drivers who had made the rush which had scattered Fanessa's forces were standing near, talking excitedly. Two policemen were on their knees by the hedge, giving first-aid to half-a-dozen men who had been injured.

One of the police had at last obtained the full story.

A barrier had been erected across the road some mile-and-a-half from Hatton airfield, and every vehicle stopped and examined. It was obvious enough that the sole purpose had been to stop Dawlish's car and rescue Lavington. Two of the men who had guarded the barrier were in police uniform, the others in plain clothes. It was obvious enough, also, that some of the attacking party had waited by the hedge until the right car came along.

As Dawlish stirred, after some fifteen minutes of unconsciousness, there was a general move back to the lorries.

Soon, the night was filled with the roar of their engines and the whining of self-starters. In a very short time only the police were left, with Dawlish and his friends, Lavington, and three members of the assault party.

'There won't be any more trouble tonight,' Dawlish said with assurance. 'We'll get on to the airfield, and you can look after these johnnies.' He spoke to the man who had driven them from Manchester.

'Very good, sir. I'll come with you to show you the way, and then bring the car back to take them into town. A fair night's work,' he added with satisfaction, 'but it looked very nasty at one time.'

'And felt it,' added Dawlish, ruefully fingering his head.

Confident that they had seen the end of this particular spot of trouble, he took his seat again, and on the short journey to the airfield considered the odds and the arrangements which had been made. Fanessa was a better organiser than he had expected, but he was puzzled by one thing.

Had it been coincidence that the barricade had been erected on the actual road they had taken?

Unless there had been a leakage amongst the police, he saw no way in which Fanessa could have selected that road intentionally, and he did not think a police leakage was likely. Whitehead had said nothing about travelling by air, and they would not have taken the same road had they been going by car all the way.

The only thing he saw as likely was that *all* roads out of the city had been watched.

That, and the fact that in spite of the depletion of their numbers at the Riall so many men had been available at the hold-up, made him think with respect of the forces at Lavington's command. The most important point was, however, that they still had Lavington and the brief-case which he had been so anxious to retain. Had he not worried about the case, thought Dawlish, he might have escaped.

They reached the airfield, and were allowed to pass through the main gates with only the briefest delay. Soon they were flying towards London.

As they circled before landing, Dawlish saw from the illuminated dial of his watch that it was not quite half-past eleven. He smiled to himself, wondering what else would happen before that day was over.

Nothing did, for when he reached Whitehall, after being brought from Heston in an R.A.F. car, Big Ben was chiming the quarter; it was fifteen minutes past twelve. With Lavington and Beresford on his right and Jeremy on his other side, Dawlish went into the building and up the stairs, on tenterhooks to learn what Whitehead could tell him.

Chapter 20

Colonel Whitehead Talks

From the moment when he had been pulled down from the hedge Lavington had not spoken. Entering the outer office of Whitehead's suite, Dawlish tightened his grip on the man's arm. He felt the other's muscles quivering, knew how much he was on edge.

The outer office, a large one, was empty. Beresford went through it and tapped on Whitehead's door.

A man nearly as tall as Dawlish, grey-haired and genial of face, Whitehead was a man whom Dawlish had come to respect very much. Often misjudged, even abused, he handled the affairs of his particular branch of counter-espionage with a precision and judgment which all who worked for him admired. It was obvious that he had come straight from his Audley Street house and the piano recital which Dawlish had heard over the telephone.

He shook Dawlish warmly by the hand, nodded to Beresford and Jeremy good-humouredly, then turned to Lavington.

'Well, Lavington?'

It was obvious to Dawlish that these men had met before.

Lavington's clothes were dishevelled, he no longer gave the impression of being something of a dandy. In the confusion of the mêlée his coat had been torn in several places, and there was an ugly bruise on his forehead. The greatest change in him, however, was the fear which lay nakedly on his face.

He spoke now in a shrill, almost inhuman voice.

'It's all a mistake, a grievous mistake. I don't understand what you mean, Whitehead. Why did you set these – these young ruffians on to me? Don't you trust me?'

'I do not,' said Whitehead quietly. He glanced at Dawlish. 'Perhaps I should explain. Lavington has been working for us for some time in Spain, and other parts of the Continent.

He has been in touch with Germany. We believed him to be a reliable and trustworthy agent, until – '

'Listen to me, Whitehead,' gasped Lavington. 'I thought that they were acting *against* us! Had I any idea that they were in your employ I would have taken them into my confidence at once. And – and I may have said foolish things when I discovered that they were more powerful than I thought, but that's the limit of it, I assure you.'

'How he talks,' said Dawlish.

'Talking won't help him,' said Whitehead, and there was a harsh note in his voice. 'We knew there was trouble in Spain and had a special investigation made. Lavington was proved to be the source of the leakage. But he skipped away before we could catch him. He's been missing for three weeks. We'd no idea where he was until forty-eight hours ago.'

Dawlish said slowly: 'Look here, I may be dull-witted, but didn't you say you hadn't even heard the name until a few days ago?'

Whitehead nodded.

'It's true enough. He was on our books as Cator. "Lavington" is a new one to me. In fact it wasn't for some time that we knew Cator and Lavington were one and the same. Once I knew the man was in England I started looking for him, but I didn't want to put you on to it just yet – you'd earned a rest,' He paused. 'I've been talking to Trivett,' he added. He stretched out a hand and touched the brown leather of Lavington's briefcase. 'I wonder how much we shall learn from this. I wonder if we shall find out where *Brunning* is.'

He uttered the word with an emphasis which startled Dawlish. In that moment all the unspoken suspicions of Posslethwaite flooded through his mind, suspicions which Lavington had fostered.

Lavington exclaimed: 'I don't know, I thought Dawlish knew. Dawlish *does* know,' he added, and there was a triumphant glitter in his eyes. 'That's where you're wrong, Whitehead. It's not I who am the renegade, but Dawlish!' He pointed a quivering finger at Dawlish, who was so startled by the outburst that he could not hide his surprise.

Whitehead smiled widely.

'That's a new idea,' he admitted.

'He's clever, he's fiendishly clever!' gasped Lavington. 'Oh, I can see it all. Listen to me, Whitehead! I admit I hid away from you, but it was because I knew what you suspected, I was afraid that I would be taken off my work. I knew that I could answer all these absurd accusations but I had to continue without interference. I managed to insinuate myself into the good graces of the most powerful Nazi organisation in this country, led by a man named Fanessa and – and someone whose name I have not yet learned, someone living in London. I became an important member of that organisation and thus discovered that Brunning is *not* in the hands of the Nazis. He is being held by English people. *Dawlish* knows where he is, Dawlish is on friendly terms with those who have him in custody. Deny that if you can!' Lavington hissed dramatically.

'He does it well, doesn't he?' murmured Dawlish.

Whitehead said slowly: 'Do you know where Brunning is by any chance?'

'Of course he does!' esclaimed Lavington. 'I tell you he's a a dangerous man. He's – '

'Be quiet!' snapped Whitehead. For a brief and unpleasant moment, Dawlish wondered if the man's words were having any effect on his Chief. 'Do you know, Dawlish?'

'I've an idea of who might be holding him,' said Dawlish.

'You don't miss much,' said Whitehead. 'Brunning is – ' He paused. 'But you probably know that too.'

Dawlish said very clearly: 'The first time I heard the name of Brunning was tonight, from Lavington. Before then I knew only that there was a man whom Lavington was anxious to kidnap.'

He knew now, as he sat back in his chair and looked at the healthy, genial figure of Colonel Whitehead, that everything turned on Brunning. The affair of Shortt, the efforts of Posslethwaite, the work of the renegade Lavington. All of those things revolved about Brunning, the mysterious man who, if Posslethwaite was to be believed, was a patient of Dr Shortt's.

The attack on the road, the desperate work at the hotel, the kidnapping of Shortt, the anxieties of Amelia and Bingham, all came back to Brunning. As he thought of this, Dawlish also thought of Posslethwaite's eagerness to keep the affair from the police: and then suddenly he saw something which had evaded him before. He leaned forward eagerly.

'Posslethwaite had a box at the Riall Safe Deposit, sir.

That's what Lavington was after there. The police are in possession of the place, but I told Posslethwaite of what had happened. He *might* send for the contents of that box, and we need it. My oath, I *am* a fool!'

'Relax, my dear fellow,' said Whitehead comfortingly. 'I gave instructions that nothing is to be taken away from the Safe Deposit until we have searched it thoroughly. There's nothing to worry about there.' He paused, then added: 'Don't you want to know about Brunning?'

'If he doesn't, we do,' said Beresford pointedly.

Lavington said in a shrill voice: 'You're wasting time, valuable time! I've spent months inveigling myself into the good graces of the enemy, but if I'm kept away much longer I shall lose all my influence. Whitehead, you must believe me, I tell you it's a matter of vital importance.'

Not for the first time, Dawlish felt an uncomfortable suspicion that Lavington *might* be right. Then he thought of all that had happened, of the numbers of men Lavington had under his control, and he dismissed the idea as absurd. Yet the man's manner did succeed in forcing doubt into his mind.

It did not appear to affect Whitehead in that way.

'Hush,' he said. 'Be quiet. We're coming to you later. Now, Dawlish – about Brunning.'

Dawlish sat back in his chair. Yet it did not ease the tension he felt, and it was obvious that Beresford and Jeremy were equally on edge.

'Brunning,' said Whitehead simply, 'was the leader of the underground movement in Germany, and we can almost say that he still is. He carries more influence than any other man in the country, outside Government officials. He has an army of saboteurs ready and waiting. He knows that he could call on what was left of the Communist and Social Democrat parties, he is in touch with all the strong elements amongst the imported labour sections in the Third Reich. We have been in regular and constant touch with him for two years. You see, Dawlish, he is a man of some consequence.'

Dawlish did see.

He had tried unsuccessfully to imagine why Brunning should be so important, but had no doubt now of the urgency and seriousness of the quest for him. Puzzles were answered; a man who could control the underground forces of Germany, even one who had a semblance of control, was a vital factor. He understood now, the imperative need to get possession of Brunning.

Nevertheless, if Posslethwaite were right then Brunning's mind had gone. If the man were found, then he would be little more than an empty husk unless Shortt's treatment was effective. Some things were answered, some mysteries solved, but the great problem remained.

It was then that Dawlish remembered, or recalled, that Dr Shortt was in the hands of Lavington and those for whom Lavington worked.

'Brunning was suspected of activities against the Reich and taken to a concentration camp,' said Whitehead quietly. 'He was there for some time, and questioned. But he was one of the few who held out. He made no confessions, implicated no one. The Nazis knew, as we did, that he had the strings of the organisation in his hands. They remain there, for no one has discovered how he worked, or with whom he worked. The most likely *successful* anti-Nazi organisation in Germany is still controlled by Brunning. Just as Hitler was a demi-god to many before his intuitions failed him, so Brunning has been the depository of all German anti-Nazi hopes. His name has been the password, and only he, in person, can really start the revolt when the time comes for it. The Germans know it, and we know it. The Germans thought they had him safe, but he escaped – or was brought away from Germany.'

'Ah, yes,' said Dawlish.

'We needn't go into how he came here,' said Whitehead, 'but he did get here. He was not – himself.' Whitehead paused a little, and added quietly: 'It was feared that nothing could mend his broken mind. But Dr Shortt essayed an attempt, and I think was making progress. Then Shortt – and you know something of this, of course – was approached by and attacked by Nazi agents over here. Lavington was amongst them: Lavington was the only man who could have connected with the German organisation and told them where to find Brunning and by whom he was being treated. I am quite sure there is no other leakage. When we knew that Shortt was being victimised we knew who started it.'

Lavington said shrilly: 'It must have been someone else, Whitehead, I know nothing of it. I've been trying to get Brunning back.'

Whitehead ignored him.

'Well, Dawlish, that is the position as clearly as I can paint it. Shortt is missing, Brunning is missing. What I don't know – or didn't know – was whether Lavington and his brood had found him. Now it's obvious that they haven't.'

'No,' said Dawlish.

Things were fitting into the right perspective in every way. He understood, now, why Lavington had talked of killing Brunning unless he could 'take possession' of him; the Germans would like Brunning back; while he lived there was a chance that they could trace the other leaders of his organisation. But rather than risk allowing the Allies to have access to that organisation, they would kill him.

Lavington, thought Dawlish, knew that he was cornered and was trying to draw suspicion on others – any others, provided he drew them all into the orbit of official suspicion. But there was a chance that he might be right about Posslethwaite: for the man in Manchester surely knew why Brunning was so badly wanted.

If Posslethwaite were to be believed, Shortt had been trying to nurse the German back to mental health: and Whitehead had confirmed that. Posslethwaite might justify his refusal to have any truck with officialdom by saying that until Brunning was mentally alive again he was of no use to anyone, and there would be ample justification for that. But there was the other thing: Posslethwaite's fear for Shortt. It might not be the turning point of the affair, it was obviously less important than Brunning's own part in it, but it mattered; until it was solved there would be no final solution.

Whitehead said slowly: 'So we have to find Brunning and Shortt. I don't think there will be much difficulty in finding Shortt, now – ' He looked at Lavington, and fingered the brief-case again. 'Brunning might be a difficult matter. It's time, I think, that I heard your story.'

He moved from his desk and called Dawlish aside. They stepped to the far end of the long, barely-furnished room, and Lavington's eyes followed them. Whitehead said in a low-pitched voice:

'Don't give away anything that he might not know. I'd like him here, he might let something fall that will help to clarify the situation. Is that all right with you?'

'Of course,' said Dawlish. There was a pleasing cunning in Colonel Whitehead's methods. It was good to feel that not

132

all the guile was on the other side.

Then he told his story.

The telling of it helped to clear Dawlish's mind of many things. It grew more than ever apparent that the only issues remaining concerned Brunning's whereabouts and the reason for Shortt's fear of the police. The others were incidental, for like Whitehead he did not think that it would be difficult to find Shortt: the brief-case would surely contain much information of interest.

Dawlish finished at last, and Whitehead stared at him steadily for several seconds.

'What an astonishing fellow you are, Dawlish!'

'Astonishing? Me?' Dawlish looked amazed.

Whitehead hid a smile.

'It's a pity that I didn't come up to see you. We must talk to Posslethwaite. You'd better go up again as soon as you've had a little rest, and I'll arrange for him and the King's Road house to be watched. Is that all right?'

'An excellent suggestion – if he's still there.'

'You fools!' exclaimed Lavington. 'Of course he will not be there, you have given him the chance to escape. Had you left it to me I would have had Brunning for you, instead you have warned Posslethwaite of official interference. Posslethwaite will now remove Brunning from wherever he is and you will never find him.'

Dawlish picked up the brief-case and turning to Lavington asked, casually, for the key. Lavington drew a sharp, hissing breath.

'You are not to open it. You mustn't open it! If you do – if you do it will be the greatest mistake of your lives"

'The key,' said Dawlish.

Without being asked, Beresford held Lavington's arms while Jeremy ran through his pockets. He held a key-case out to Dawlish, without speaking. Dawlish in turn handed it to Whitehead. The case held about a dozen small keys, and slowly Whitehead chose one of them. It did not fit.

'Stop that, stop it!' gasped Lavngiton, every vestige of colour drained from his face. 'I tell you it must not be opened!'

Whitehead ignored him and tried another key.

'It will kill us all!' gasped Lavington. 'No one in the room will be alive if you open it! It must be kept locked!' He shrieked the words while staring at Whitehead, his eyes starting from his head. There was perspiration on his forehead, and his lips were quivering.

As Whitehead tried another key, Lavington made a convulsive movement forward; he would have reached the desk had not Beresford shot out an arm and grabbed his coat.

'It's madness, madness!' shrieked Lavington. 'You'll kill us all!'

He began to mutter gibberish, running words into one another, but his manner was such that he made Whitehead pause and look thoughtfully across at him, made even Beresford and Jeremy frown in uncertainty, and caused Dawlish to eye the case with some anxiety.

Whitehead tried a fourth key; it fitted the lock perfectly. He kept it between his finger and thumb and looked at Lavington, who continued to shout and rave and down whose face beads of perspiration were falling in quick succession.

Chapter 21

The Lies Of Lavington

Whitehead did not give the impression that he was greatly affected by Lavington's raving, but it remained a fact that he did not turn the key. Beresford looked at the shouting man, trying to make up his mind whether Lavington's frenzy was genuine or a superb piece of acting.

The man was now clutching Dawlish's arm.

'Stop him, Dawlish! Stop him!'

'I think, sir,' said Dawlish much more formally than usual, 'that it would be best if I were to take the case to a place where it can do no harm, on the chance that it is as lethal as Lavington suggests.'

Whitehead raised his eyebrows.

'You are suggesting that you take the case somewhere where it can only do harm to yourself when you open it?'

'And Lavington,' corrected Dawlish gently.

'I won't go with it,' shouted Lavington. 'I've warned you, and I won't go with it!'

Beresford spoke for the first time since entering the office.

'Not your job, Pat. Mine.'

'I don't agree,' said Jeremy lazily. 'Mine.'

'The thing is, you're of more use than I am,' Beresford went on, 'and if it blows me to Kingdom Come I'll have no major complaint – provided Lavington comes with me.'

'That was my idea, originally,' said Jeremy with some feeling. 'Tell you what, Ted. We'll toss for it.'

'You damned fools!' shouted Lavington. 'What is there to joke about, what is so funny? I tell you no one will live within – within a hundred yards of it if that case is opened!'

Beresford took a silver coin from his pocket.

'Heads or tails, Tim?'

'Don't waste the effort,' said Dawlish. 'I'm dealing with this.' He looked at Whitehead. 'That's if it's all right with you, sir, although actually I don't think it's going to cause as much trouble as Lavington makes out. My guess is gas, so a gas mask should be a good enough protection. Why not carry the test out in one of the air raid shelters?'

'It's crazy,' said Jeremy quickly. 'Damn it, Pat, you're worth a dozen of either of us. I mean, ask the Colonel. Distressing thing to have to admit, but –'

Dawlish chuckled.

'True recognition at last, but I think we've taken too much notice of Lavington, and I'm sure we're losing too much time.' He raised an eyebrow questioningly towards Whitehead, who left the key in the case and answered quietly:

'I don't mind whether it's Beresford or Jeremy, but as I can't do it I'm not going to let you, Dawlish.' He smiled a little ironically. 'There it is, so we won't have any more argument.'

So it was that Beresford spun his coin while Jeremy called 'heads'. The coin, revealed on the back of Beresford's hand, showed tails upwards.

It was just ten minutes later that Jeremy entered a small air raid shelter built in the courtyard of the Whitehall building, accompanied by Lavington. Both were wearing gas masks.

The others stayed inside the building.

Dawlish had both hands thrust deep in his pockets. He knew that Whitehead was right enough. False modesty was pointless. Whitehead believed that he, Dawlish, would be of more use to the Department than either Beresford or Tim Jeremy, and since there was obviously a risk that the case contained some kind of explosive he was taking no unnecessary chances.

A faint light, in the shape of an 'S', pin-pointed the shelter. Dawlish could just see it as he stood by the side of a window. Whitehead and Beresford stood near him, hidden figures in the darkness, their presence revealed only by their breathing.

Once Beresford heaved a quick sigh.

Dawlish looked at the illuminated dial of his watch, and said suddenly:

'Two minutes. That's quite enough, if the key was the right one it needn't have taken five seconds.'

He did not wait for any order from Whitehead, but hurried along the passage and through the open door leading into the courtyard. Beresford was close on his heels. Dawlish would not have been surprised to see the sudden flash of an explosion, but that did not make him slacken his footsteps. Then, when he was within ten yards of the shelter, shining his torch to the entrance, he saw a figure lurching away from it.

It was Jeremy, pulling at something on the floor.

In a moment Dawlish had reached him, and lifted him clear. Beresford dived past him, seeing the head of Lavington close to the ground. He gripped the man's shoulders, and lugged him away.

Dawlish, meanwhile, saw the brief-case clutched in Jeremy's hand. The flap was open, but there appeared to be no papers. There was a faint smell, growing stronger as the moments passed. Dawlish guessed what had happened.

There had been a release of gas when the case had been opened, and the gas had been of a type against which gas masks were not effective. He felt a sharp, deep fear for Tim Jeremy, a fear so personal and vivid that for the time being at least all else was swept from his mind.

*

Dawlish, back in Whitehead's office, put the case on the Colonel's desk. His face looked strained and bleak. Beresford was not with them; he had gone in an ambulance which had taken both Tim Jeremy and Lavington to the Central Hospital. The shelter was roped off, wet blankets were draped over the exit and the ventilators, and any attempt at cleansing the place had been postponed until further knowledge had been gained as to the type of gas used. An expert from the Home Office was going to the hospital, and from where a report was expected at any moment.

Whitehead, his face a little drawn, said slowly: 'There isn't a great deal that you miss, Dawlish, is there?'

'There's enough,' Dawlish said. 'If Tim goes – ' He drew a deep breath, and then said evenly: 'I suppose we ought to have a look inside now?'

Together they opened the case fully, taking out a number of manilla folders and two slim loose-leaf books. Dawlish paid them less attention for the moment than he paid to the little gadget fitted to the lock of the case.

It was a small metal container, and he saw that as the case opened, so the container opened too, and the gas was released. He noted the mechanism by which pressure at a certain point of the lock fitting would have kept the container closed. Only Lavington or someone who knew how to manipulate the case could have known that.

Whitehead put the papers in an orderly pile in front of him, and pushed the books towards Dawlish.

'You start on those,' he said briefly.

Dawlish opened the first book, and saw an ordinary loose-leaf filling, with an index. He turned to 'R', and the third entry, with a page to itself, concerned the Riall Hotel. It held a list of the men who worked there, giving proof of what he had suspected – that although a genuine hotel five days out of six, on the sixth it was used exclusively for Lavington's purposes. Fanessa was listed as 'Manager'.

'Not bad for a start,' thought Dawlish.

It grew better. There were a number of hotels up and down the country where similar arrangements held. Whenever it was necessary for arrangements to be made for a conference, or for Lavington's presence, the hotel was 'closed'. The dates when the places had been taken over were noted down; some had been in the hands of the Lavington organisation for ten years, others – like the Riall – only for a matter of months. The main reason for taking over the Riall had been because it was next door to the Riall Safe Deposit; there was a footnote here, saying: *See Posslethwaite.*

Dawlish glanced up at Whitehead, who seemed lost in his inspection of the papers. Shrugging, Dawlish turned to 'P', and found a full page on Posslethwaite. He read through a brief biography of the man, and then read on with even deeper interest:

Actual motives not known. Deep interest in Shortt, whether or not for personal reasons remains uncertain. Interest equally deep in Brunning. Undoubtedly knows where Brunning is held but has refused bribes up to £1,000 to disclose information. Discovered that his private papers are in the Riall Safe Deposit, Manchester, Box 103 (see Riall Hotel). Obviously fully cognisant of Shortt's past, adamant in refusing to disclose it to the police. Doubtful whether actuated by friendship for Shortt (although a patient who has benefitted from the Shortt treatment). Probably for personal profit. Attended by Owen Richard Jones, old servant and laboratory assistant. Jones possibly corruptible but not where Posslethwaite is concerned as far as can be dis-

138

covered. Jones passionately devoted to Posslethwaite, might be best approached by threat or injury to the man. (See Jones.)

There was nothing else of exceptional interest, and Dawlish looked up, this time to find Whitehead staring at him intently.

'Well, Dawlish?'

'Lavington's in deep,' said Dawlish, 'and we shouldn't have a lot of trouble in closing down his particular branch of the game. And we should be able to find Brunning.'

'Yes,' said Whitehead. 'If he's still alive.'

Dawlish said: 'Why shouldn't he be?'

'There's a note here suggesting that he's dead,' said Whitehead quietly. 'It's dated the day before yesterday, so it seems to be fairly up-to-date.'

Dawlish said slowly: 'And how much does it really matter?'

'Far more than I can say,' said Whitehead with an underlying note of emphasis which clearly denoted his belief in the vital part which Brunning could play in the break-up of Nazi Germany. 'There is no single man of such importance, Dawlish. If he's dead – '

Whitehead paused, and then went on:

'If he's dead, it might mean a period of three, even six months added to the war, it will delay or prevent the arrest of thousands of the worst members of the Nazi Party, it will probably condemn to death tens of thousands of pro-Allied workers in Europe. You see, Dawlish – Brunning is not only the leader, but as far as we can tell he's the only man who can *name* these agents. There's a list of them somewhere. If we can't save Brunning then we might be able to do something if we can only get hold of that list, although it's more than probable that they'll work only on Brunning's instructions. Do you follow?'

'Only too well,' said Dawlish slowly.

'And Brunning might be dead,' said Whitehead again.

'Who was that report from?'

'It's signed by a man who calls himself "Smith", and there's no address. We won't be able to get much from that. But we've got to find out the truth. We must be sure whether Brunning is alive or dead.'

The telephone rang. Whitehead stretched out a hand for the instrument.

Dawlish sat back, half-closing his eyes.

He wished that he did not feel so physically tired. He knew that he had plunged into this affair before he had fully recovered from the weariness which the big effort of the past week had caused, and to keep his head clear and to devote his fullest and best attention to the affair of Brunning he needed sleep: he glanced at his watch and saw that it was half-past one. If he could be in bed by two o'clock, by eight he would wake up feeling refreshed and capable.

Whitehead was saying: 'Are you quite sure? . . . What time did you say? . . . Five minutes to one. . . . What about the man Jones? . . . I see – '

'Jones,' murmured Dawlish. 'Posslethwaite.' He no longer had to fight against weariness, for the moment he was as alert as he could wish. He confounded the way Whitehead kept asking trivial questions. But his Chief replaced the receiver at last, and Dawlish, waiting for him to speak, felt quite sure that Posslethwaite was dead.

Chapter 22

Back At Clay House

Whitehead turned, and spoke very deliberately: 'Your Mr Posslethwaite has gone, Dawlish.'

'Gone?' echoed Dawlish blankly. 'How do you mean, "gone"?'

'No one seems to know,' said Whitehead heavily. 'He was at King's Road at half-past twelve, presumably asleep and certainly in bed. At five to one he was discovered missing, his bed empty. Jones, sleeping in the next room, claims to know nothing about it.'

'Oh,' said Dawlish.

'It begins to look as if Posslethwaite was foxing you. And others, too, for that matter,' said Whitehead. 'The infirmity couldn't have been as bad as he made out.'

'Possibly not,' admitted Dawlish. 'But Jones has been nursing him, so he wouldn't be easily fooled.'

'You've said that he's passionately devoted to the other man,' Whitehead pointed out, 'so there's the possibility of collusion.'

'Yes,' admitted Dawlish. 'I think I'd like to see Jones.'

'I'll have him brought down here,' said Whitehead. 'But before you do anything else you're going to have a good night's rest. You look tired out.'

Dawlish smiled.

'And I feel it! However, there are other things. Lavington is sure that the information about Brunning's hiding-place is contained in Box 103 at the Riall Safe Deposit – Posslethwaite's box. That ought to help.'

'If it's true.' Whitehead made a note on a pad in front of him. 'Box 103. I'll have it brought down here. Now off you go.'

Whitehead had sent for a car, and it was waiting in Whitehall when Dawlish reached the street.

The journey to Clay House in the blackout took nearly

twenty-five minutes, and Dawlish spent the time alternately dozing and thinking. There was an unpleasant feeling in the pit of his stomach when he contemplated Whitehead's theory about Posslethwaite. He did not want to believe it, but the possibility that it might be true had to be faced.

He was no further on in his thoughts when the car pulled up outside the main doors of Clay House. Two minutes later Dawlish entered the darkened hall. The girl on night-duty eyed him brightly from behind the reception desk.

'Why, Major Dawlish! I'm very glad you're here, Lieutenant Hubbard has been very anxious to see you. Shall I tell him that you're on your way upstairs?'

'Yes, please,' said Dawlish. 'Where is he?'

'In the small lounge, with Miss Shortt and – ' She glanced down at a notebook. 'A lady named Deverall.'

'Ah, Felicity,' said Dawlish, his eyes kindling.

The small lounge door was open, and it widened as he drew nearer. Amelia Shortt hurried forward, tumbling over Hubbard's foot in her excitement. Beyond, Dawlish caught a glimpse of Felicity. She was in uniform, and looked towards him with a smile which made the world a different place for Patrick Dawlish.

Amelia flung her arms about him, uttering little squeals of delight. Evading her with some difficulty, Dawlish advanced towards Felicity.

'Hallo, my sweet.'

'Pat.' She gripped his hands. 'Oh, Pat,' she said again, and turned him so that he was able to see into a mirror.

He had not had an opportunity to tidy himself since the rough-house on the road, and in the course of that he had grown considerably dishevelled. It was not this, however, which held his attention, but the lipstick smudges on both cheeks.

Ruefully he took out a handkerchief.

'Oh, don't worry about that!' said Amelia breathlessly. 'Felicity won't mind. Sit down and tell us *every*thing. I can't really believe that you've been so wonderful, you – '

'Now steady,' said Dawlish. 'We've managed to get you out of immediate harm, but that's about our limit.'

'Oh, nonsense!' declared Amelia. 'It's only a matter of time now. I can't imagine why it was we waited so long before asking you to help.' There was only the faintest hint of anxiety in her voice as she went on: 'Pat, you will get my

142

father back, won't you?'

Dawlish looked at her speculatively.

She was as breathtakingly lovely as ever; it might have been early evening instead of something after two o'clock. There was no doubt that her vibrant vivacity eclipsed Felicity. Yet it was to Felicity's grey-green eyes and restful personality that he constantly turned.

'You will, won't you?' demanded Amelia with a slight increase in the tension of her voice.

With repeated reassurance Dawlish managed to escape from the room, taking Felicity with him. He left Hubbard and Amelia still talking, the sailor appearing to have no objection to staying up all night.

Outside his door, Dawlish stopped, and there was a smile in his tired eyes.

'The parting of the ways again, my sweet.'

'Not for much longer,' said Felicity. She kissed him lightly. 'How is the job going, darling?'

'No more than fair. I think you'd be better than I would at softening up Amelia. Will you do that for me? I want to learn why her father is afraid of the police – and why *she* is, for that matter. Gently will do it, we don't want to stampede her. Apart from that – well, it's a matter mostly of waiting.'

'Of course I'll do what I can. Where's Ted, and Tim?'

Felicity saw the expression in his eyes alter, and her own smile faded.

'Are they all right?'

'Ted is. Tim's not so good. We'll know more by the morning. I'll tell you all of it tomorrow, once we've got rid of Amelia.'

'Hubbard will look after her,' Felicity said with assurance.

As Dawlish climbed into bed, he was preoccupied with the fact that Felicity was so certain about it. It was not the romantic aspect which worried him – although he was by no means sure that any man would be happy if he lost his heart to Amelia. What gave him cause for thought was the fact that Hubbard had attached himself, voluntarily, at the beginning of the affair. He had wondered once or twice whether the sailor had any ulterior motive, and decided that it was unlikely. Now he found himself wondering whether Hubbard and Amelia were old acquaintances, and her part in this tangle deeper and more tortuous than it appeared to be.

In the fog between sleeping and waking he was depressed and uncertain.

That feeling remained when he was awakened soon after eight o'clock and told that Miss Deverall had asked her to call him.

Bathed, shaved and dressed, he sped towards the breakfast room, meeting Felicity on the way.

'Hallo, there.' He tucked her arm beneath his. 'Why the early bird act, Fel? I'd hoped to have time for at least two more cups of tea, and another half-hour snooze before breakfast.'

'Whitehead wants you at the office at half-past nine,' Felicity told him. 'He didn't say why, but he was anxious that you shouldn't be late.'

'Ah. That looks like business. Nothing else?'

'I've 'phoned Ted,' said Felicity as they entered the breakfast room. 'He's heard that there's a little better chance of Tim pulling through.'

'Thank God for that,' said Dawlish with feeling. 'Any news of Lavington?'

Felicity shook her head.

'Hm. What about Amelia?'

'Oh, she was full of talk last night, we didn't go to bed until three o'clock. Such vitality the girl has! I have to report that she is disappointed in you.'

Dawlish's lips curved.

'I can hardly bear it. Nothing else?'

'Hubbard's fallen for her,' said Felicity simply.

'Hm. Are they old friends?'

'I don't think so.' The question seemed to surprise Felicity. 'At least four others here are in the same boat, but she's not really interested in any of them. Her only real interest seems to be in her father. Do you know where he is?'

'Not yet,' said Dawlish, 'but it's probably only a matter of elimination.'

There was a pause while the waiter drew near with various hot, covered dishes. When he had padded off again Dawlish said:

'Has Amelia mentioned the name Brunning?'

Felicity considered, and then shook her head.

'I don't remember it. Who is he?'

'The whole affair turns on him,' said Dawlish. He launched into a brief résumé of the affair while Felicity listened, silent

144

and grave-faced. As a clock struck nine-fifteen, Dawlish leapt to his feet.

'I'll come over with you,' Felicity said, 'I've a report to make, anyhow.'

It was when they were in the passage, about to approach the steps, that they heard a scream.

It came from the first floor, above their heads, a woman's voice raised in fear, perhaps in pain. A second cry, earsplitting enough to make a dozen people rush into the hall, followed swiftly. Dawlish raced for the stairs.

He heard footsteps, and a man's voice shouting. Then he reached the landing.

Amelia was lying half-in, half-out of the doorway of the small lounge. Bending over her was a powerfully-built man, whose hands were about her throat. Dawlish could only see his back, yet knew in a moment who it was.

A wheelchair, standing empty in the passage, was confirmation, had he wanted it; the man trying to strangle Amelia was Posslethwaite, and Hubbard was trying to drag him off. Dawlish reached the scene, caught a glimpse of Amelia's eyes bulging from her head, saw her tongue protruding between her lips.

Dawlish shouldered Hubbard aside, gripped Posslethwaite's wrist with an expert pressure which made the man's hands fall away. He lurched to one side, his whole body in a state of extreme collapse.

Gently, Dawlish released him.

Hubbard was on his knees by Amelia. Felicity was giving crisp orders to the crowd which had gathered. In a few minutes Amelia was in her room, carried there by Hubbard and another man, and Felicity was with her. Posslethwaite lay inert, breathing very faintly.

Dawlish thought desperately: He needs an injection, Jones is the only one likely to have the stuff. Unless – He began to go through Posslethwaite's pockets, heedless of the watchers, intent only on what he was doing. Pen, pencil, watch, keys he dropped on the floor, one after the other, and then, reaching the hip-pocket with great difficulty, he found a small cardboard box.

Inside was a hypodermic syringe, fully charged.

He hesitated for a moment, looked into Posslethwaite's face, saw the eyes open, glazed and lack-lustre. He held the syringe up and said sharply:

'Is this right?' A pause. *'Is it right?'*

He believed that Posslethwaite would die unless he received the right injection, knew that it was a gamble which might not come off, but which he had to take. He stared into those lack-lustre eyes, his whole body tense. That Posslethwaite must not die until he had explained much more than he had done so far, was the only thing that mattered.

Then Posslethwaite nodded.

'Ah,' ejaculated Dawlish.

He knew that he might still be wrong, that Posslethwaite might want to die: but it was a chance he must take. Vividly he remembered how Jones had made the earlier injection. He prepared the skin as best he could, and drove the needle home.

Posslethwaite sagged back against the chair.

For the first time Dawlish became aware of the many curious glances sent towards him from residents at the Leave Club. He straightened up, smiling a little for effect and not because he felt in any way amused. There had been problems enough before, but he had thought that with the discovery of Brunning and the explanation of Shortt's 'skeleton' nothing else of importance would be revealed. He had been wrong. The pressing question now was: why had Posslethwaite tried to murder Amelia when in Manchester he had shown himself so staunch a supporter of the girl?

It could be that Posslethwaite had made a discovery which had led to the *volte face*, a discovery which implicated Amelia. Dawlish did not want Amelia implicated, there was enough confusion already. Frowning, he stepped towards the door, intent on finding out how the girl was. Before he reached it, it was flung open and Bingham rushed in, wild-eyed, dishevelled, haggard.

'Dawlish!' he exclaimed thickly. 'Dawlish, where's Amelia, where is she? She's in great danger! I must warn her. *Where is she?'*

Chapter 23

The Contents Of Box 103

Dawlish would not have been surprised had Bingham burst into tears. The man seemed to be at the absolute limit of endurance. He stared wildly into Dawlish's eyes, repeating the question without giving Dawlish a chance to answer.

Dawlish said sharply: 'Amelia's all right. Take a hold on yourself.'

'She isn't, Posslethwaite's after her. He's sworn to kill her, he's sworn to. He – '

'He doesn't look much like killing anyone,' said Dawlish, and stood aside so that Bingham could see the man from Manchester.

Bingham rose to his full height.

It was a peculiar moment, for Dawlish seemed to see a man who was regulated by strings or some unseen mechanism. Bingham's mouth dropped open, his arms rose and fell by his sides, his eyes widened, narrowed, widened again. All the time he was taking in deep gulps of air. It was a queer demonstration, striking a note so odd that Dawlish was intrigued in spite of himself.

'P-P-Posslethwaite!' gasped Bingham. 'Here! He – '

'Now steady,' said Dawlish, gripping the youthful doctor's arm. 'Posslethwaite can do no more harm, and I'm pretty sure that he missed with Amelia.'

'Missed?' echoed Bingham. 'What do you mean, missed?' His voice rose upwards to a shriek. 'Dawlish, is she all right? Is she all right?'

'Be quiet,' snapped Dawlish.

He spoke harshly but no more so than he felt. Men whose voices lost control – shrieks and mutterings, incoherences, whispers, gasps – he was tired of them. No one behaved normally for five minutes on end. The only really sane man whom he had met had been Posslethwaite – until a short while before. Now Posslethwaite had joined the others, was classified with them. None of them were normal.

Dawlish thought with a sudden alarm: Of course not. They're all treating – or being treated as – abnormal cases.

Momentarily he felt a chill of doubt, of alarm, even of fear. There had been abnormalities, eccentricities from the very beginning. He might solve straightforward problems but those organised by unhinged minds were beyond his range.

As quickly as it had come the feeling faded. Something took its place – a vague suspicion at first, developing into conviction as Bingham stood gasping and gaping at him. Too many people were *pretending* to be unbalanced. Lavington, Bingham, Posslethwaite and Jones. The pitiful little naked man at Mere Street, Professor Anstey. Even Amelia, who was either in the throes of deep excitement or the depths of gloom. There was no normality about any of them; even Fanessa had the same touch. Carter – just the thug Carter – was the only man who had acted without giving the impression that he was unbalanced.

Aloud, Dawlish said: 'Operative word, pretending. I wonder – '

'Who's pretending?' screamed Bingham. 'Where's Amelia? If you don't tell me where Amelia is I'll – '

He broke off in turn, for Dawlish, filled with the new idea and developing it as he went along, drew Bingham into the passage. He was not surprised to find Hubbard approaching from one of the other rooms. He looked harassed, but not altogether upset.

'Hallo, Pat,' he said, casting a curious glance towards Bingham. 'She's all right now – nothing serious.'

'Amelia?' shouted Bingham.

Hubbard stared at him more intently.

'Amelia Shortt, yes,' he said.

'So she is all right,' gasped Bingham. 'She's all right. Oh, thank God, thank God!' He brushed his hand across his forehead. His corn-coloured hair was damp against his brow. 'I was afraid she – she would be killed, like her – ' He broke off abruptly, his lips quivering. 'Poor Amelia. Did she suffer much, Dawlish?'

Dawlish said deliberately: 'Not as much as you're going to.' He fastened his grip on Bingham's arm. 'Hub, will you go to the flat, and tell Ted that I'll be there soon, bringing Bingham with me?'

He looked up, to see Felicity hurrying towards him. She had just come from Amelia, who was recovering consciousness. It appeared that Posslethwaite had arrived in his wheelchair and asked to see Amelia, who had been in the small lounge. His chair had been taken up in the lift. A maid had seen Amelia open the door and welcome Posslethwaite, who had then, with a tremendous physical effort, risen from his chair and attacked her.

'Posslethwaite must be mad,' Hubbard said angrily.

'Mad? Of course he is!' exclaimed Bingham. 'I don't blame him in some ways for what he did, he couldn't know that Amelia only arranged it for his own sake, and her father's, of course. It – it's really very simple, Dawlish.'

Dawlish looked at him steadily, before turning away.

'We must have different ideas on what constitutes simplicity.'

He did not leave Clay House until Whitehead had sent men to look after Posslethwaite, and also Amelia. Whitehead said nothing about why he had wanted to see Dawlish, but agreed that the interview had best be postponed.

Felicity, Bingham, Hubbard and Dawlish took a taxi to the Brook Street flat.

There Ted Beresford was awaiting them.

Dawlish said no further word of the theory which was already developing in his mind, a theory that much of the fuss had been created for the sake of it – some of the demonstrations of temper and insanity deliberately staged so that he should be deceived. He did not know how many – if any – had been genuine, but that some of them had been faked, he was increasingly sure.

They crowded into the flat.

Bingham sat in a chair with Beresford on one side of him, Hubbard on the other. Dawlish stood with an elbow on the mantelpiece, looking down at the man from his great height. On the journey Bingham had been subdued, and now he looked apprehensively into Dawlish's eyes.

'What are you looking at me like that for?' he demanded tensely. 'What's the matter, Dawlish?'

'Your ideas of simplicity,' said Dawlish slowly.

'But – but it is, Dawlish, it is simple! Posslethwaite has been a good friend of Dr Shortt's, and of Amelia's. He has kept certain details away from the police, for instance, and he has refused to betray Dr Shortt's special patient to *any*-one.'

That was reasonable, thought Dawlish, and was not at difference with anything he already knew.

'I don't know who this special patient is,' said Bingham earnestly. 'Very few people do, but he's most important, Dawlish, I do know that. Posslethwaite was faithful, but – well, it's time the authorities knew. I mean, you *had* to know. You're one of the Intelligence Department, aren't you?' Bingham paused.

Dawlish gave a brief nod, surprised at the extent of the other's knowledge.

'There you are,' said Bingham triumphantly. 'Posslethwaite wouldn't tell you, he preferred to keep the man's name entirely to himself, and I can tell you this, he had all the particulars in a box at a safe deposit in Manchester. But perhaps you already knew that,' he added, darting a quick look at Dawlish. 'The thing is, he was going to destroy the box. I heard him say so. I knew the number, and where it was kept. He said that if he couldn't use the contents himself, he'd make sure that no one else did. But – ' Bingham drew a deep breath. 'Amelia knew where it was, and also the number, and she had a key – it used to belong to her father, you see. She gave me the key, and I went over last night and took everything out of the box.'

Bingham did not appear to notice the growing tension. He spoke earnestly, even portentously, preening himself a little, quite sure that he was the central figure, and rather liking it.

'Go on,' said Dawlish quietly.

'Having got hold of the contents I held on to them for a bit,' said Bingham self-righteously. 'However, I made the mistake of telling Jones what I'd done. Jones told Posslethwaite, who knew that Amelia was the only other person to have a key, and so – so he came after her.' Bingham swallowed. 'Posslethwaite's not really sane, anything unusual is liable to send him crackers. I had a call in the early hours of this morning telling me that he'd managed to get away from Manchester, and was after Amelia. So I got down here as fast as I could – I've travelled all night,' he added with a little laugh. 'I expect I look a bit of a mess. I had good reason for being scared, you see.'

'Yes,' said Dawlish. 'Where are the contents of the box?'

Bingham stared at him.

'Why, don't you know?'

'Now look here – ' began Dawlish, only to be cut short as Bingham said explosively;

'*Your* Chief has them, of course – Whitehead. I've read about some of your other affairs, Dawlish, and Whitehead's name appeared in them. So I took them straight to Whitehall and asked for him. He saw me himself, I'm quite sure it was Whitehead.' He broke off, then added a little peevishly: 'I don't see what more you could expect.'

Dawlish drew a deep breath.

'No,' he admitted. 'No, I don't see, either.' There was a thoughtful smile on his lips. 'I'm doing well, and Whitehead's doing better. He has all Lavington's stuff, all Posslethwaite's, and a pretty good story in the bargain.' He eyed Bingham in silence for a few seconds, and then added very softly: 'Where's Brunning, Bingham?'

Bingham stared.

'Who? Who did you say?'

'It doesn't matter,' said Dawlish, 'But if you don't know where Brunning is, you can tell me where Dr Shortt is, can't you?'

Bingham gaped at him.

'What *are* you talking about, Dawlish? Why, I'm *looking* for him!'

'No,' said Dawlish deliberately.

'But – but I tell you – '

'Where's Shortt?' snapped Dawlish, and leaned forward to seize Bingham's wrists. He caught them in one great hand and held the man helpless in his grip. 'Don't lie and don't argue! Tell me where Shortt is!'

Bingham began to mutter incoherently again, his tongue running along his lips.

Dawlish said cuttingly: 'You know where he is. You've done your damndest to whitewash yourself, but it isn't working. *Where's Dr Shortt?*'

Beresford and Hubbard stared at Dawlish as if they thought that he had taken leave of his senses. Only Felicity looked as if she had faith in the big man as he peered close into Bingham's eyes. Except for the man's harsh breathing there was no other sound in the lounge.

'Waiting won't help you,' said Dawlish after a long pause.

'I – I've no idea, no idea at all,' gasped Bingham. 'I can't see how you think I know anything Dawlish.'

Dawlish said: 'I think you're in this up to the neck, Bingham. I think you've been the go-between for Lavington and Fanessa, and then with Posslethwaite and Dr Shortt. *Someone* had to tell Lavington and Fanessa where to find Brunning, or where they might find Brunning. You did that, and – ' He broke off suddenly, his face, grim enough already, taking on an even bleaker look. 'Why, yes,' he added harshly, 'you'd seen the contents of the box before you handed them over to Whitehead, and you made quite sure that you extracted the information you needed. Who did you send it to? Don't talk to me about not knowing Brunning – who did you tell where to find him?'

Bingham gasped: 'No one, Dawlish, no one, you're wrong, quite wrong!'

Dawlish snapped: 'Was it Fanessa?'

'No, no, I don't know anyone. I couldn't have told anyone. I took the box straight to Whitehead – '

'You simple-minded fool,' said Dawlish scathingly. 'My name has appeared in the papers often enough, but never Whitehead's *as my superior officer*. You couldn't have had access to Whitehead's name unless you knew a lot more than you pretend. That's item one. And item two – you say that you *hurried* down from Manchester either by road or by a night train, actually you took seven or eight hours at least, and all the time if you're to be believed you knew that Posslethwaite was coming after Amelia. You didn't telephone a warning, you came down and lost hours, and you even went to Whitehead before going to Clay House. Then you arrived and pretended to be frantic. Operative word, pretended,' he added harshly. 'It hasn't worked, Bingham. Who have you told about Brunning's hiding place?'

Bingham made no denials, said nothing at all. But the frenzy had gone from his expression, there was a colder, more cunning glint in his eyes. Dawlish was quite sure that he was right about the man, equally convinced that Fanessa knew now where to find Brunning. The box had been stolen, the necessary information obtained, and then Bingham had tried to cover his part in it by a show of honesty and good intentions. That did not matter now, the truth was plain enough for himself and the others to see. The crucial fact was that Fanessa, or one of his gang, *knew where to find Brunning*.

Dawlish said in a low-pitched voice: 'If I have to shake the life out of you I'll learn the truth.'

Bingham said nothing.

Dawlish leaned forward, menace in every line.

'Tell me, Bingham, where can I find them?' He was thinking desperately: Fanessa or some of Lavington's men know, they'll get there first. Brunning dead will be better for them than a Brunning alive and in our hands. If they can't abduct him they'll kill him. He might even be dead now. He felt cold perspiration on his forehead, remembered how definite Whitehead had been, was convinced of the vital importance of saving Brunning's life.

He left Bingham alone for some seconds, lit a cigarette, appeared to ignore the fact that Bingham was there, and thrust his hands deep in his pockets. Bingham's breathing grew easier, and he settled himself more comfortably in his chair. Dawlish noted the crafty glitter in the man's eyes.

Suddenly he sprang from his chair, proving that he had not been so exhausted as he had pretended.

He reached the door and pulled it open, but Dawlish was close upon his heels, pleased up to a point because Bingham had now made a virtual confession of guilt and swept all possible doubts away.

Bingham reached the hall door.

Dawlish said over his shoulder: 'Go out the back way, you two, and follow him. He'll have to lead us where we want him to.'

In fact, Dawlish knew, there was no 'have to' about it. He was taking a chance, yet saw no other way in which the situation could be handled.

Bingham pulled open the outer door, and rushed towards the stairs. And then Dawlish saw a man coming up them, a man whose very existence he had forgotten for at least twelve hours past.

Superintendent Trivett of Scotland Yard was blocking Bingham's path.

Chapter 24

One Stage Further

After the first moment of mortification Dawlish turned his attention to another factor, one which surprised him and made him forget his own disappointment. That was less acute because he had been by no means certain that he could be sure that Bingham would lead him to any significant place quickly enough. Dawlish knew that speed was all important. If Brunning was still alive, he had little doubt that the man had never been in such great danger as he was now.

The other factor concerned Trivett.

He was not surprised to see the Yard man: on the contrary he knew that Trivett might well have been expected to show a further curiosity, for he would know that Dawlish had not been idle. The surprise came in the fact that Trivett and Bingham recognised each other.

Moreover, Bingham made it apparent that he was as frightened of Trivett as he had been of Dawlish.

The whole gamut of impressions came and went in a few seconds, before Bingham took what must have seemed to him the most obvious course and charged full tilt at Trivett – much in the way that Lavington had done in Manchester. The difference was that Trivett was prepared for it. He gave way a little under the impact, and then shot out his left hand in a swing which brought a gleam of admiration to Dawlish's eyes. For Trivett's fist cracked against the side of Bingham's jaw, flinging the yellow-haired doctor against the head of the stairs.

Bingham, who made no attempt to get up, lay gasping and muttering as Dawlish went forward.

'Hallo, Bill,' he said admiringly. 'I've rarely seen a better one than that.'

Trivett rubbed the knuckles of his right hand gently.

'What an astonishing chap you are, Pat.'

'What, do you think so too?' asked Dawlish incredulously. 'For the first time in my life everyone seems to be gathering round me with loud hurrahs. What have I done this time?'

Trivett glanced at Bingham, and said: 'I've put a general call out for him less than an hour ago.'

Dawlish stared at him, facetiousness quite gone.

After the way Trivett had looked, and the power which he had put into his punch, he should not have been surprised. Yet 'surprised' was a mild word for what he felt. He had dreamed of many things, was quite certain that Bingham, by over-acting his part had given himself away. The fact that the man had rushed to try to escape had proved to his satisfaction that he was implicated, but Dawlish had been prepared for trouble in proving it. Now Trivett told him calmly that he had a general call out for the man, that the police wanted Bingham badly: unless they had some weighty evidence against him they would certainly have not taken such strong measures.

Trivett said lightly: 'Don't tell me you didn't realise it.'

'I realised he was up to no good,' said Dawlish faintly. 'But I didn't think I'd get your support so easily. Bill, nothing in this show has gone as I expected it to. Why you had to choose this moment to come here I don't know. Coincidence don't they call it?'

Trivett shook his head.

'Nothing so chancey as that, I've had a man watching the flat for twelve hours, and he 'phoned a short while back to say that you'd returned. He didn't mention Bingham, but he wasn't after Bingham anyhow. Hadn't we better get inside?'

Dawlish stooped over the prostrate man, and dragged him to his feet. He moved ahead unprotestingly.

Dawlish made his way to the lounge. He was a worried man. The urgency had not decreased, but there was an added difficulty. Trivett had first claim on Bingham, and he did not think there was any chance at all that Bingham would respond to police interrogation.

But he did not allow his anxiety to reveal itself, did not want to give anything away to Trivett. He was relieved that Trivett seemed so good-tempered. It would not have been surprising had the Superintendent considered that Dawlish had bamboozled him.

At sight of Trivett, Ted and Hubbard looked somewhat

disconcerted. Trivett's handsome face relaxed in a dry smile.

'Three guilty consciences,' he said. 'As a matter of fact, Pat, Colonel Whitehead had a word in your favour with the A.C., so you've nothing at all to worry about. But how on earth did you manage to get hold of Bingham?'

'He grew careless,' said Dawlish, and then something clicked home in his mind. Sharply, he went on: 'Why do you want him?'

Trivett, in the act of lighting a cigarette, said gently: 'So you don't know that? I think you've had more luck than is good for you, Pat! I want him for the murder of the servant, Kibb, at Dr Shortt's house. The knife was found,' he added, 'and Bingham's prints were on it. We discovered that Bingham had been there about the time of the murder, and one way and the other are quite sure he's our man. The evidence will stand up in court all right, too.'

Dawlish said slowly: 'Well, well. What about the motive? Do you know it?'

'Not yet,' admitted Trivett regretfully.

'The motive,' said Dawlish softly. 'If we can find that out, we'll be even further on in this business than we have been before. Where have you looked for him, Bill?'

Trivett frowned.

'I don't follow you.'

'His flat, of course. And his surgery?'

'Oh, I see,' said Trivett. 'Yes, we've looked in all the obvious places, but he hasn't been there. We telephoned Manchester, for we learned from one of the other doctors at the surgery that he had gone north for some reason or other. Does it matter?'

Dawlish eyed him without speaking for a few moments.

The room was very silent. Beresford and Hubbard did their spectator acts without any appearance of resentment; it did not occur to Dawlish until afterwards that they had been onlookers for most of the time. Nothing occurred to him then except the fact that Bingham must know where Brunning was, that Bingham had told others, that the others almost certainly included Fanessa and that Fanessa would kill Brunning at the earliest opportunity. It crowded most of the other considerations out of his mind. He felt frustrated, impotent, angry with himself. He must find out where Brunning was hidden, must get going again, yet there was no way of seeing through the brick wall with which he was confronted.

He said abruptly: 'Bill, did Hubbard ring you and ask you whether you'd ever come across the man Fanessa?'

'Of course I did,' put in Hubbard.

'Yes,' said Trivett. 'He's a second-rate music-hall artiste, a fortune-teller in a big way. We've had our eye on him several times, but he's always kept on just the right side of the law. That's about all we know about him.'

'All,' said Dawlish, and smacked one clenched fist into the palm of his other hand. 'There must be something else, Bill, it can't end there. Where does he live?'

'At a small club in South Kensington,' said Trivett. 'One of those clubs for hangers-on in the theatrical world, used mostly for getting drink at all hours. Why?'

Dawlish said slowly: 'South Kensington. Are you sure?'

'Yes, but – '

'Get the address,' implored Dawlish. 'Get it now, and – well, you know the address of Bingham's surgery, don't you? There's just a chance – ' He stopped, and appeared to stare at Trivett as the latter, taking his point and asking no further questions, stepped towards the telephone.

Actually Dawlish was watching Bingham, and he saw a change come over the youthful doctor.

He was looking covertly at Trivett, his eyes sharp and alert. Again Dawlish felt sure that the man had feigned the frenzy, pretended the collapse; there was much cunning in Bingham. Trivett lifted the telephone, and as he began to dial, Bingham moved from his chair like lightning and charged towards the policeman. Quick though Dawlish was in his wake Bingham reached the telephone and jerked it out of Trivett's hand, then tried to pull the cable from its socket. He did not succeed, for Dawlish reached him first.

'Do we want any more telling?' he demanded harshly. 'Bill, look after Bingham, and have some men sent to the surgery at South Kensington. Don't lose any time. Perhaps – ' He paused, pushed Bingham a yard away from him, and then without hesitation brought his clenched fist up to crack against the man's chin. Bingham fell backwards, his eyes rolling.

'He shouldn't cause you any more trouble,' said Dawlish. 'Ted, go down and get a cab. No, two cabs, Bill will want one. Help him, Hub.' Dawlish spoke as he moved towards

157

his bedroom, and he disappeared inside as Beresford and Hubbard, the latter a little confused, went to the front door. For a moment Trivett stood indeterminately with the receiver in his hand, then he dialled Scotland Yard.

Dawlish, coming out of the bedroom with two automatics, paid him no attention but hurried in the wake of his friends. When he reached the street, the two taxis were approaching.

One driver was told to wait for Trivett: Dawlish, Beresford and Hubbard bundled into the other, giving the address of the surgery near South Kensington Station.

Then, and only then, did Dawlish relax.

He felt quite sure that Bingham had wanted to prevent the telephone call for only one reason – to gain time for Fanessa. There was only a slight doubt, a possibility that Bingham had done what he had in order to set them chasing in the wrong direction; but he doubted whether the man had sufficient guile for that.

'Look here, Pat, what *are* we going to do?' demanded Hubbard at last.

'Raid the surgery,' said Dawlish quietly. 'I don't think Fanessa's club will be far away from it, in fact it might be at the same address. And a great deal now turns on Fanessa.' He looked out of the window, seeing that they were approaching Kensington High Street. At the back of his mind there was a fear that they might be too late, that, by now, Brunning might be dead. The confusion of thought and the crying need for getting Brunning were heavy on his mind.

They approached the underground station.

Beresford opened the glass partition between the driver and the rear of the cab, and gave instructions. They turned into a side street, went along for fifty yards, then turned again, finding themselves in a dingy thoroughfare with a few shops on either side.

The taxi stopped outside a single-fronted shop. On the door was a brass plate containing the names of three doctors, Bingham's at the foot. The door to the shop, apparently a self-contained one, was almost adjacent to another door leading to a flight of stairs. On a board on the second door were several names, and amongst them a declaration to the effect that the *Second Arts Club* would be found on the first and second floors.

'Well I'm damned!' exclaimed Hubbard.

'There's plenty of time for that,' said Beresford. 'What's first, Pat?'

Dawlish said quickly: 'Hubbard, get round to the back and force your way in. Be careful, because – ' He hesitated only for a moment, then thrust one of the automatics into the sailor's hand. 'Guess why,' he added briefly. 'You can cut across that patch of bare ground. Ted, you get into the surgery somehow or other, and stop anyone from coming out.'

'Right,' said Beresford.

He did not wait to ask what Dawlish proposed to do, while Hubbard was already hurrying towards the rear of the surgery and the club. The taxi driver, who had instructions to wait, simply stared at them in silent astonishment.

Dawlish put his shoulder to the door leading to the *Second Arts Club* and found that it opened with little difficulty.

Beresford was at the surgery door, but Dawlish did not give him a second thought – he knew the other had his service revolver and that he would be even more capable of prompt action than Hubbard. Dawlish concentrated on the club premises, the conviction that Fanessa used them as his headquarters, anxious lest the place was deserted.

He found himself in a narrow passage, leading to a flight of stairs. He went upwards steadily, arriving at a small landing, with three doors leading from it. He heard no sound, no indication that anyone had heard him coming. He hesitated only for a moment before opening the first door; it led to a bathroom. The second was littered with empty glasses and cigarette ends. A combined smell of stale beer and tobacco smoke made him wrinkle his nose in distaste. Behind a narrow bar was an array of bottles, most of them empty.

The third door was locked.

Dawlish put his shoulder to it: the flimsy lock gave way with little trouble, and Dawlish was precipitated inside. It was a lounge, comfortably furnished, with the same stale atmosphere as the other room.

It was not empty, however: a white-haired man was lying on a settee, bound hand and foot.

Chapter 25

The Rescue Of Dr Shortt

As he advanced towards the settee he had a feeling of anti-climax. It did not occur to him that this man might be Brunning. He wished that he recognised him, but set that thought aside as he unfastened the gag at the other's mouth.

He heard footsteps from somewhere below him, and thought that they were probably Hubbard's; there was a sound of breaking glass, and he suspected that Beresford had found the only way to get into the surgery was to break the glass of the door.

The man on the settee drew in a deep, gasping breath of air. Dawlish took a knife from his pocket and cut through the cords binding the victim's wrists, then did the same to the cord at the ankles. That done, he left the room to return with a glass and a jug of water from the bar. The man gulped down a little water gratefully. His lips were so stiff that he could hardly speak, but he did manage to croak:

'Who – who are you?'

'Dawlish,' said Dawlish briefly. 'Who – '

He did not finish the question.

Quite suddenly, and so vividly that he did not really understand why he had been so long arriving at the conclusion, he realised who this was. And the thought was hardly in his mind when the other said hoarsely:

'Shortt – I am Dr Shortt.'

'Well, well,' said Dawlish absurdly.

He had succeeded in at least half of what he had set out to do. Vaguely thoughts of what Posslethwaite and others had said of the ability of this man flashed through his mind. If they were right then Shortt would spell sanity to hundreds, perhaps thousands of people.

Yes, thought Dawlish, it was a triumph in its way, *but Shortt was not Brunning*.

Shortt went on in the same cracked voice: 'Have – have you got him?'

160

'Who?' asked Dawlish quickly, although he thought he knew the answer. 'Who do you mean?'

Shortt gasped: 'Brunning – Brunning, of course. You must find Brunning, he – he is in great danger. Fanessa – '

Brunning and Fanessa, it all came back to them. Dawlish felt a crazy impatience, yet knew that impatience would get him nowhere. He said in a low-pitched voice:

'Where is Brunning?'

'He was – here,' croaked Shortt. 'He was here. Not long ago.'

'Not long ago,' repeated Dawlish blankly, 'but is he here now? Where's Fanessa, do you know that?'

'No,' said Shortt. 'No. But you must find Brunning, you must find – '

The door below crashed open, and footsteps leapt up the stairs. They were those of three or four men. Dawlish thought at once of the police, but even as he stepped to the door of the room, he knew that he was wrong.

From below there came a loud call:

'Pat! Look out!'

That was Beresford, thought Dawlish. He dashed out to the landing, gun in hand. He heard Beresford call out again, but this time the cry was strangled, dying away in a low gurgle. It was muffled by the thunder of the footsteps, and Dawlish saw the leader for the first time.

He thought: So it's Fanessa.

He had already passed Dawlish, and was half up the second flight of stairs. Two other men followed him. They were armed, and Dawlish wondered why they did not shoot. He pressed the trigger of his own gun. In the narrow landing the roar reverberated like a cannon, and the nearer of the two men stopped in his tracks, swayed, and then fell forward. The second man fired as the other fell, and Dawlish felt the impact, then a burning pain in his left shoulder.

He fired again.

The bullet struck the other's right arm, sending the gun flying from his grasp. It happened very quickly, and then the man flung himself bodily at Dawlish. He leapt to one side, but though he could not evade all the force of the impact, he retained his grip on the gun.

He brought it down on the back of his assailant's head, barrel first. The man gasped. A second blow made him relax his grip and slither to the ground.

Dawlish was alone but for the two men on the floor, and Shortt in the room behind him, too helpless to move.

Other sounds were coming from upstairs. Dawlish realised that Fanessa was trying to break down a locked door. Dawlish stepped towards the stairs, but he felt unsteady, the pain in his shoulder was acute and agonising. He tightened his grip on his gun, and began to climb upwards, while the thunder on the unseen door grew louder.

Dawlish rounded a bend in the stairs.

It was then that he saw Fanessa again, beating against the door of a room, flinging his whole weight against it. The man seemed oblivious to anything else. Dawlish went up slowly, his shoulder, arm and chest feeling warm and wet.

He was sure in his own mind that Brunning was in the room beyond.

At the head of the stairs Dawlish stood and levelled his gun; but his hand would not keep steady. He gritted his teeth, and went forward a step. In spite of his frenzy Fanessa was making little impression on the door.

Steadying himself against a banister, Dawlish fired.

Fanessa swung round, his face livid. Suddenly there were other sounds, footsteps on the stairs, loud voices, and another warning cry, this time from Hubbard.

'Pat – Pat – '

Fanessa had been using the butt of a gun to beat at the door. Now he turned it in his hand and fired at Dawlish: and he did not miss, the bullet sent Dawlish reeling backwards. There was a second shot, this time from behind him. Fanessa gasped, and dropped his own gun.

'Pat!' called Hubbard, and there was a note of desperation in his voice.

Dawlish guessed that Hubbard was being attacked. He heard no more than one man on the stairs behind him. Then he reached Fanessa, who was swaying in front of the door.

Dawlish did not know that Hubbard was at the landing below, facing three men who were coming towards him. He was kneeling in front of the body of a third and was wounded in the chest and the arm. Yet he had his gun and fired again, trying desperately to gain time for Dawlish.

Dawlish saw Fanessa slump towards the ground. He had no strength left to batter at the door ahead of him, but Fanessa had done that part of his work well. As Dawlish put his hand against it, it sagged open.

Dawlish staggered inside. His mind was clear enough, and he could see a man lying on a narrow bed.

The man's hair was dark and overlong, and he was unconscious.

The room might have been that of a nursing home; it was white and clean. Dawlish felt sure that the man was Brunning.

Suddenly, warningly, Hubbard's voice reached him.

'Pat, they're coming!'

Dawlish stepped further into the room and closed the door behind him. Even the closing of it took a considerable effort. He looked about him desperately, saw a small chair within reach. He pulled it towards him as a bullet struck a panel of the door, passing within two inches of Dawlish's shoulder. Desperately he blocked the door with the chair.

There was a strange moment of silence.

The black-haired man on the bed did not stir, and from outside the room there was no noticeable sound. Then a voice said clearly:

'Open the door, Dawlish. We don't want to hurt you.'

Dawlish said nothing. He did not know how long the chair would withstand the pressure, his one thought was to get the man on the bed to a place of safety. Had he been uninjured he would have tried the window, but that was now impossible. Everything stood or fell by whether he could keep the door blocked for a few minutes longer.

Minutes, thought Dawlish, that was all. Trivett's men would be here soon, it was hard to understand why they had not arrived before. Minutes, between him and Brunning and complete disaster.

The thunderous banging on the door jolted the chair forward. Dawlish looked about him, saw a small dressing-table, but doubted whether he had the strength to drag it to the door; he wondered whether it would be of much use if he succeeded. He decided that it would not, and stepped towards the bed, where the man there lay unconscious, not moving, oblivious to all that was happening so close to him.

It was then that Dawlish heard a car draw up outside.

At first it meant little – it was just a car. Then he heard voices and the crack of revolver shots. There was an increase in the frenzied banging on the door of the room, but he did not pay much attention to that. He managed to get to the window in time to see two other cars draw up and plainclothes policemen jump from them.

There was an ominous splintering sound. Dawlish turned, and saw that one of the legs of the chair had broken, the door would not withstand much more pressure. He found a reserve of strength which he had not suspected to be within him, and flung his whole weight against it, leaning forward, knowing that if shots were fired they could not miss him. He felt the panels quivering beneath the onslaught on the other side, but then heard footsteps, a voice which he believed was Trivett's. He did not know what happened next, did not see the man who had been hammering against the door rush towards the police, nor the fight which followed. He stood gasping for breath, nausea coming over him in waves. Then vaguely he heard Trivett's voice again. He forced himself away from the door, staggered and would have fallen but for the wall.

Trivett came in, stopping short at the sight of Dawlish who was hardly recognisable.

Dawlish croaked: 'That's him – I think. Brunning. Don't let anyone – '

'All right, Pat, all right,' said Trivett in a reassuring voice which sounded a long way off. 'There's nothing to worry about now. Take it easy.'

'Easy,' muttered Dawlish. 'Take it easy.'

Brunning found, he felt sure: and Dr Shortt. The two men they wanted so badly. Bingham caught, Fanessa outside and helpless, Lavington perhaps dead. It was all over, there was nothing more to worry about, and yet –

He was not satisfied.

He did not know why. He only knew that there was something else that he badly wanted to know, and he could not think what it was. He thought of Amelia and Hubbard. He thought of Dr Shortt and all that Posslethwaite had said of him. Shortt, who had a black record which must be kept from the police. Shortt – Posslethwaite – Jones. And Posslethwaite had tried to kill Amelia. There was no doubt about that. Was it because of the stolen box? Was that the reason?

He was vaguely aware of people moving, of being put on a stretcher. It was surprising how gently they treated him, he thought. He warned them again about Brunning, remembered that he was not really sure that the black-haired man was the German.

It *must* be, it had to be.

Suddenly, it was cold and very bright, and he realised that he was in the street. He narrowed his eyes against the sun, and then saw a strange party coming towards him. At first it seemed like a mirage, it was so absurd.

First of all there was Whitehead.

By Whitehead's side, pushing a wheelchair, was little Jones with his comical face set and tense. By Jones's side was Amelia Shortt.

'It's crazy,' muttered Dawlish. 'Quite crazy.'

Posslethwaite was in the wheelchair. The queerest thing, quite the most absurd thing in the whole cameo, *was that Amelia was holding Posslethwaite's hand.*

'I'm dreaming,' thought Dawlish, as he was put on the pavement, the stretcher being lowered without any jolting. He saw that another stretcher was being brought from the house, and just caught a glimpse of a head of black hair. He looked at Whitehead and framed a question which he could not utter, but Whitehead was not returning his gaze. Then he grew aware of a deep voice, and of Posslethwaite's eyes looking at him with a humorous gleam in them.

'Aye, you're reet,' said Posslethwaite. 'That's Brunning, Dawlish.'

So it is Brunning, thought Dawlish, and experienced a wave of relief which did not altogether hide the fact that he was troubled by something else, something he could not properly understand.

Chapter 26

Clouds Cleared Away

After the bullet had been removed from his shoulder, Felicity was Pat Dawlish's first visitor.

She did not talk for long, but assured him that everything was being well-looked after, that Lavington was dead and that Tim Jeremy was going to recover, that Beresford had nothing more than heavy bruises to worry about, that Brunning was now with Shortt, who was back at his house. That Posslethwaite and Amelia were on very good terms – Dawlish was more puzzled about that than anything else – and that Hubbard, a little disconsolate, was coming to the conclusion that between Amelia and Posslethwaite there was a bond greater than he was ever likely to forge with her.

Felicity let him know all those things and yet contrived to do it so that they dawned upon him only in recollection, when she had gone. He dozed a little, musing over the puzzle of Amelia and Posslethwaite. The essentials were over, that was a comfort; but there was the problem of Shortt. It harassed him, but did not prevent him from having a good night.

Next morning the problem remained as insistent as ever.

Dawlish was much improved, although he knew that it would be several days before he was able to leave the hospital, and that whatever was done about Shortt would be arranged without his help, perhaps without his knowledge. Amelia came, bright-eyed and cheerful, kissing him without restraint and telling him that she had known from the start that he was wonderful. Little Jones came, bringing a posy of flowers; then Ted looked in, with nothing more deadly than a black eye and a cut over his right temple.

They were all very cheerful, but not informative. Dawlish began to feel restless. There was something he did not understand, he felt that there was a conspiracy of silence and was not convinced that it was only because he was a patient in hospital. There were undercurrents which he could not fathom.

He forgot about it when Felicity came to see him, but when she had gone it came back again.

Shortt – Posslethwaite – Amelia.

It was on the second day of his convalescence that Whitehead came, bringing Trivett with him. Dawlish was sitting up in bed, his shoulder and arm heavily bandaged, but feeling much more like his old self. His eyes brightened when the two men entered the ward, and he said promptly:

'The invalid's fine, but he's also curious. How has it worked out?'

Whitehead pursed his lips.

'Well, we've finished going through the papers in the brief case, and there isn't a great deal outstanding. Lavington was the leader of the organisation, Fanessa – an Italian by birth and a fascist by conviction – was the second-in-command. They hoodwinked us nicely for a while; Fanessa once worked on our staff.'

'I knew his name was familiar,' exclaimed Dawlish.

Whitehead waived the comment aside.

'They had this hotel chain up and down the country, with a large staff which evaded internment rather cleverly. Then Brunning reached England, and went to Shortt – '

'Who sent him there?' asked Dawlish.

'We did,' said Whitehead ruefully. 'We knew of Shortt's experiments, were assured that he was the only man who might cure Brunning. Only Posslethwaite, Bingham and Jones knew of it. Bingham, who worked only for money, gave the secret away, and made it possible for Lavington and Fanessa to get to work. Bingham was trying to find out where Brunning was hidden – he was actually in a north-country nursing home. Then Brunning was kidnapped and brought to the Club, where he had medical attention from Bingham. Lavington and Fanessa wanted to get him back to health and then smuggled out of the country, you see. They thought they would get away with it right up to the last minute. Bingham tried to cover himself. Incidentally he killed Kibb because he was known by Kibb to have lured Shortt into the hands of Lavington and company.'

Dawlish pursed his lips, then said: 'Repeat.'

Whitehead frowned a little.

'I'll put it this way. Bingham was one of the party that

167

kidnapped Shortt. Kibb knew that, and had to be killed.'

'Who asked for me?' asked Dawlish. 'Bingham said – '

'Amelia was solely responsible for that,' Whitehead assured him. 'She knew that her father was restless and worried, managed to get a garbled version about blackmail. Bingham encouraged that idea, playing what he thought was a clever double game. Lavington, who forgot to keep Bingham informed of all that he was doing, sent those spoof telegrams – we've a note of it in his books.'

'But why?' demanded Dawlish helplessly.

'His notes say that he believed that if he got you to Mere Street he could put you, Posslethwaite and Jones away at the same time – he thought you might be dangerous, Pat, particularly because you worked with the Department.'

'Yes,' murmured Dawlish, although by no means satisfied.

'Posslethwaite was in Shortt's confidence, as was Jones – up to a point. Then Bingham obtained the box from the safe deposit and opened it, found where Brunning was, and arranged the kidnapping. Posslethwaite learned of that. It turned his mind – he has periods of dementia. He knew that Bingham had obtained the key from Amelia, believed Amelia a party to it, was obsessed by the need for getting at her. He came down by ambulance, which Jones arranged. When Posslethwaite's mind cleared and he was able to understand that Amelia had given the key to Bingham only because she was convinced that Bingham wanted to help, he – well, we needn't go into that. There was a reconciliation. You probably remember –'

'They were holding hands, yes,' said Dawlish. 'I suppose Amelia is prepared to consider as a suitor a man whose mind might collapse at any time.'

Whitehead said quietly: 'Amelia knows what we all know now, Dawlish. Posslethwaite won't live for long. He's holding on because he wants to see Brunning recover. After that –' Whitehead shrugged. 'Amelia is being kind, Dawlish.'

'But it's not in keeping with her character,' said Dawlish doggedly.

Whitehead said nothing, but Trivett murmured: 'Aren't you prejudiced, Pat?'

Dawlish said vehemently: 'I'm prepared to believe that Amelia will be as loyal as they're made if she thinks the circumstances warrant it, but unless she's in love with Posslethwaite she wouldn't pretend anything different. She doesn't

168

care for anyone but her father. To Amelia, Posslethwaite would appear an uncouth, rough-voiced plebian. Don't have any doubt about that. Amelia has some other motive, and it shouldn't be hard to find.'

There was silence for a few moments, and then Whitehead spoke ruefully.

'Well, I admit we're not *quite* satisfied. And yet –'

Dawlish said: 'Why was Shortt afraid of the police? Or hasn't that been divulged?'

Trivett said slowly: 'It's an old affair, Pat. Shortt needed money for his experiments many years ago, and employed a man to forge a substantial cheque for him – a cheque on the account of a man who died shortly afterwards. It was cashed without question, but Shortt found that it preyed on his mind. He told a few people, including Posslethwaite. It was a long time ago, and there is no evidence. In the circumstances –'

Dawlish looked at him steadily. Trivett broke off, and Whitehead went on:

'Shortt is the one man who might save Brunning.' He paused. 'That's the most important thing at the moment.'

Very slowly, very definitely, Dawlish shook his head.

The others stared at him, but Dawlish did not immediately speak. When he did it was to ask for a cigarette. Trivett supplied it, Whitehead lit it. Dawlish drew in a deep breath of smoke, exuded it slowly, and murmured:

'Weakness number one – something you've forgotten. Bingham on the one hand, Fanessa and Lavington on the other. Two separate parties working for the same thing. Bingham knew where Brunning was but *after* he had the information Lavington was still looking for it. So Bingham did not tell Lavington, obviously.'

Whitehead stared, and Trivett's lips tightened.

'A fact,' said Dawlish. 'No doubt about it. Posslethwaite had charge of Brunning, and presumably moved him from place to place. Bingham found the last place and reported, but Lavington – or rather Fanessa – didn't learn from him. Who did?'

'Go on,' said Whitehead quietly.

'Who was with Brunning?' demanded Dawlish. He paused and then added gently: 'We've been taken in quite a lot over this business. Fake fits, fake friendships, fake everything. Why not a fake kidnapping? *Was* Shortt kidnapped? Or did he go voluntarily, realising that when Amelia persuaded me to come into it I might stumble on his real part?'

'But – ' began Trivett, and then stopped abruptly.

'Go on,' repeated Whitehead.

'Bingham pretending to have quarrelled with Shortt made it look as if Shortt was genuinely kidnapped,' said Dawlish. 'Everything depended on that. Shortt made up a fake story about a forged cheque to provide a plausible explanation of his reluctance to go to the police. Supposing he was reluctant only because he was afraid to? He would persuade both Amelia and Posslethwaite of that, but Amelia probably knows the truth by now, that her father, working behind so many covers, is actually the leader of this organisation, or I'm quite crazy. Amelia is afraid that Posslethwaite knows, puts herself out to placate him. There's only been one real attachment for Amelia, only one that's shown. That for her father – and praiseworthy enough. She'll do anything for him. Anything. And she's doing this.'

Trivett said in a practical voice: 'Is it anything more than guesswork, Pat?'

Dawlish answered sharply: 'Does anything else answer everything? Shortt is known as the specialist in this mind-cure business. Men whose minds have turned through torment in Germany get here – and we send them to Shortt. He hears all they say, he's in a position to send everything they say abroad. Brunning was the most vital factor. He had, somehow, to keep Brunning. It grew obvious that the organisation might crack, because Posslethwaite was causing trouble. So he started Lavington and Fanessa working in the open, he put the whole tortuous business into operation, and the others were loyal enough to their accursed Third Reich to suffer anything to let him get away with it. Lavington died rather than help us. Bingham damned himself rather than let us gain an unnecessary minute. Fanessa waited until the absolute last minute, when it was obvious that Shortt wasn't safe. Then, only then, was Brunning better dead than alive.'

'But why wasn't Shortt safe?' demanded Whitehead.

'Because we were bound to find him at the Arts Club,' said Dawlish. 'Oh, they tried everything, even putting a fake note in their records saying that "Browning" was believed dead – remember? They thought that I suspected our precious Dr Shortt, they thought it was all up. Then when it was over Shortt found himself an object of sympathy. Amelia would say nothing. Posslethwaite – well, I don't really believe he knows. Amelia is just playing safe.'

Whitehead said slowly: 'I don't see any way of proving this, Dawlish, even if there is any truth in it.'

'There must be a way,' said Dawlish, his face flushed with the exertions. 'There must – '

It was then that the door of the private ward opened and Ted Beresford came in with Felicity.

Beresford said slowly: 'We missed plenty, Pat.' He did not look at the others, but spoke directly to Dawlish. 'We missed Shortt. I was with Posslethwaite and Amelia, visiting Brunning at Shortt's house. Actually I went to prise Hubbard away, he was making something of a fool of himself over Amelia and I wanted to try to discourage him. Posslethwaite asked to see Brunning, and Shortt tried to stop him. Posslethwaite flew into a rage. I got there in time to stop Shortt from killing Posslethwaite and Amelia – he was about to use that gas, the same stuff that was used with Lavington.'

Ted paused, but there was absolute silence in the ward.

'I caught the phial and it didn't break,' he went on, conjuring up in Dawlish's mind a picture sublime in its heroism. 'Shortt broke down. Then Posslethwaite discovered why Shortt wanted to prevent him from seeing Brunning – *Brunning was sane.* Shortt didn't want us to learn that until he had the information Brunning could give him. Brunning has told me where to find this, the complete list of his people in Germany. It is hidden in the rooms he rented when he first came to England. Amelia – ' Ted paused. 'She suspected something of this, I think. She's prostrate. I feel damned sorry for that girl, Pat.'

After a long pause, Dawlish said: 'Yes. So do I. The gas, of course, that's what it all turned on. There was some in the laboratory, Shortt thought I found it when I was hunting around there, believed I would be on to him since the same stuff was used on Lavington's brief case.' He looked rueful as he went on: 'It's so easy to miss the obvious, but you've got your evidence, Bill.'

Beresford stared at him.

'Do you mean you had any idea of it, Pat?'

'There wasn't any other answer to everything,' said Dawlish, simply.

Whitehead looked at him, his expression a strange mixture

171

of admiration, exasperation, and gratitude.

'You'll do,' he said. 'One way and the other it hasn't worked out badly at all. I think you and I had better go and get the ends tied up, Trivett. You won't be long, Beresford, will you?'

'No,' said Beresford a little absently, and looked at Dawlish. 'Pat, I give you up. I'd no idea at all.'

Dawlish chuckled.

'At one time nor had I. I'm still wondering what would have happened had Bingham escaped instead of running into Trivett.' He stifled a yawn. 'Hallo – going already?'

He put his arm round Felicity, and at her touch neither heard nor noticed the door close behind his friend.

THE END

A SELECTION OF FINE READING AVAILABLE IN CORGI BOOKS

Novels

☐ 552 98247 4	THE HISTORY OF THE NUDE IN PHOTOGRAPHY (illustrated)	Peter Lacey and Anthony La Rotonda	125p
☐ 552 98345 4	THE ARTIST AND THE NUDE (illustrated)		105p
☐ 552 08069 1	THE OTHER VICTORIANS	Steven Marcus	50p
☐ 552 08664 9	THE HUMAN ZOO	Desmond Morris	35p
☐ 552 08162 0	THE NAKED APE	Desmond Morris	30p
☐ 552 08611 8	FEEDING THE FLAME	T. Lobsang Rampa	30p
☐ 552 08765 3	THE HERMIT	T. Lobsang Rampa	30p
☐ 552 08630 4	BRUCE TEGNER'S COMPLETE BOOK OF KARATE (illustrated)	Bruce Tegner	40p
☐ 552 98479 5	MADEMOISELLE 1 + 1 (illustrated)	Marcel Veronese and Jean-Claude Peretz	105p
☐ 552 08807 2	BIRTH CONTROL NOW AND TOMORROW	Clive Wood	30p

Western

☐ 552 08532 4	BLOOD BROTHER	Elliott Arnold	40p
☐ 552 08813 7	SUDDEN AT BAY	Frederick H. Christian	25p
☐ 552 08841 2	BAD HOMBRE	J. T. Edson	25p
☐ 552 08706 8	SLIP GUN No. 65	J. T. Edson	25p
☐ 552 08783 1	HELL IN THE PALO DURO No. 66	J. T. Edson	25p
☐ 552 08840 4	UNDER THE SWEETWATER RIM	Louis L'Amour	25p
☐ 552 08673 8	NORTH TO THE RAILS	Louis L'Amour	25p
☐ 552 08802 1	No. 9 THE DEVIL'S MARSHAL	Louis Masterson	20p
☐ 552 08803 X	No. 10 GUNMAN'S INHERITANCE	Louis Masterson	20p

Crime

☐ 552 08824 2	A PUZZLE IN PEARLS	John Creasey	25p
☐ 552 08739 4	TRAITOR'S EXIT	John Gardner	25p
☐ 552 08809 9	MADRIGAL	John Gardner	25p
☐ 552 08782 3	THE LITTLE WAX DOLL	Norah Lofts	30p
☐ 552 08640 1	RED FILE FOR CALLAN	James Mitchell	25p
☐ 552 08758 0	SURVIVAL ... ZERO!	Mickey Spillane	25p
☐ 552 08839 0	TOUCHFEATHER TOO	Jimmy Sangster	25p
☐ 552 08801 3	THE SILENT LIARS	Michael Underwood	25p

All these books are available at your bookshop or newsagent; or can be ordered direct from the publisher. Just tick the titles you want and fill in the form below.

— —

CORGI BOOKS, Cash Sales Department, P.O. Box 11, Falmouth, Cornwall.

Please send cheque or postal order. No currency, and allow 5p per book to cover the cost of postage and packing in U.K., and overseas.

NAME ....

ADDRESS ....

(NOV '71) ....